S.T.E.M.

SQUAD

BLACKOUT:

Danger in the Dark

All inquiries should be addressed to:
Barron's Educational Series, Inc.
250 Wireless Boulevard
Hauppauge, New York 11788
www.barronseduc.com

ISBN: 978-1-4380-0921-6

Library of Congress Control Number: 2016025600

Date of Manufacture: August 2016
Manufactured by: B12V12G

Printed in the United States of America

9 8 7 6 5 4 3 2 1

BLACKOUT:

Danger in the Dark

Aaron Rosenberg
Illustrated by Deb Gross

S.T.E.M.

SQUAD

Julie Robbins

Malik Jamar

Christopher Wong

Tracey DeGuerra

Ilyana Desoff

CHAPTER 1

STAYING CURRENT

"Oh, come on!" Julie "Jules" Robbins complained as the lights flickered. "Not again!" She sat back with a groan and waited. Her backpack lay open on the bed next to her, and there were piles of clean clothes beside that, but how was she supposed to figure out what to pack if she couldn't see what she was doing?

She heard footsteps out in the hall. Then a knock on her door. "Yeah?"

Her father cracked the door open enough to peek in. "Everything okay, sweetie?" he asked. As always, he filled the entire doorway, blocking out the light from the hall. But Jules was pretty sure that light was wavering as well.

She gestured up at her ceiling fan, and the lights there, blinking on and off. "If you call this okay," she answered.

Her dad sighed. "I know," he answered. "We had a few brownouts at work today, too. And there've been blackouts in the area all week. This should pass, though." Sure enough, the light steadied again, almost as if it'd heard him. Jules giggled a little at that thought and the accompanying image of her big, strong, no-nonsense dad scolding the lightbulbs until they behaved.

A **brownout** is when the voltage drops in an electrical system. This causes the lights within that system to dim. Brownouts can be deliberate or accidental.
A **blackout** is when an area loses electrical power. Blackouts can be short term, lasting only a few minutes or hours, or long term, lasting days, weeks, or even months.

Just then, the doorbell rang. "Are we expecting any packages?" Jules looked up, surprised. Who would be at their door at this hour? But her dad smiled. "Ah, that'd be Dustin," he said, already heading for the stairs.

Curious, Jules followed. She could finish packing later. She stood at the top of the stairs and watched as her father answered the door. "Hey, Dustin, come on in. Thanks for coming."

"Hey, no problem, Joe," Dustin Negavi replied, stepping inside. "Hey, Jules," he called up when he saw her. "How's the shoulder?"

"A little sore, that's all," she answered with a smile and a wave. The Negavis had been their neighbors for years, and their son Dwayne was Jules's age—they'd actually played on several co-ed teams together. The Negavis had moved away a year or two ago, into a different neighborhood, but the two families still got together when they could—and often went to each other's games. Which was why they'd been there at her basketball game yesterday and had seen her hit the floor after one tussle for the ball. It had hurt, but Jules had been lucky—nothing was broken or even sprained; it was just a few aches and bruises and scrapes.

"I asked Dustin to stop by," Jules's dad explained as she came down the stairs to join them, "just to make sure these brownouts and blackouts aren't messing up our wiring or anything."

"Always a good idea to check," Mr. Negavi agreed. "Just to be safe."

Jules had forgotten that their former neighbor worked for the electric company. "What's your job, exactly?" she asked. Mr. Enright would want to hear all about this, she figured.

Mr. Negavi looked pleased at the interest. "I'm an electrical engineer," he answered. "I help install and check electrical components, like the wiring in your house or the fuse box."

"What's that?" Jules asked next, indicating the object in his hand. It looked like a really big, thick phone or an oversized TV remote, except that it had a big red plastic clamp at the top.

"Oh, this? This is my multimeter," Mr. Negavi told her. He held it up for her to see. There was a single big dial just below the clamp, and a digital readout below that, followed by four round plugs like for a headphone. "I use this to measure electrical current, voltage, and resistance."

Voltage is the difference in electrical charge between two points.
Current is the rate at which charge is flowing.
Resistance is a material's resistance to current.

"Cool." Jules followed along as her dad led Mr. Negavi downstairs to the fuse box. "How's it work?"

"It's pretty simple, really," the electrician answered. He glanced around their basement, which was set up as a family room, and nodded when he spied the outlet over by the TV on the far wall. "First, I need to make sure the meter's working correctly," he explained. He pulled out two wires, a red one and a black one, each with a thick plastic handle near the top, just below an exposed wire tip. "These are my leads." He plugged them into two of the ports at the bottom of the meter. Then he tapped the dial—Jules saw that it had several settings on it, one of which read "Off." "I turn the selector switch to DC Voltage, like so," Mr. Negavi told her, twisting the dial to the lower of the two "V" settings, which had what looked like an equals sign next to it. He set the meter on the floor next to the wall outlet. "Then I touch both leads to the socket. I just have to be really careful not to let the leads touch each other—if they do that, they'll short circuit." He carefully tapped the red lead into the longer of the two vertical slots in the socket and the black lead into the shorter one. The digital readout remained blank. "That's fine," he explained. "Outlets use AC, alternating current, rather than DC, direct current, but I still need to check, just to be safe."

Then he switched the dial to the upper "V," which had a wavy symbol beside it. "Next, I measure the AC voltage," he said. This time the readout lit up, showing 118.8. "Great. It should be at or near 120, so that's perfect."

Then he went over to the fuse box itself, bringing the multimeter with him and removing the two leads as he walked. He opened the fuse box and studied the rows of circuits there. "We just need to check the voltage here now," he told her and her dad, who was standing just a few feet away, watching silently. "I do that with the clamp—all I have to do is pull out the conducting wire a little"—he reached in with one of the disconnected leads and tugged a wire loose near the bottom of the box—"and then clamp onto that." He latched the clamp onto the wire, and immediately the readout lit up, this time showing 121.1. "Great. That means you've got a good, steady voltage here, which is exactly what we want. Now I just need to check the current." He turned the dial to where it said "A" with a squiggly line, then attached the clamp again. Now the readout showed 12.2. "That's just a little over 12 amps," Mr. Negavi told her. "That's fine. These are 15-amp breakers, so they can handle up to 15 or a little more. Your whole house can handle around 200 amps at a time, spread out through the various circuits here."

"So we're good?" Jules's dad asked.

"Yep, all good," the electrician replied, shutting the fuse box and putting his multimeter away. "If a house has old wiring or faulty connectors, the sudden shifts in current caused by brownouts and blackouts could damage the electrical systems. Everything here is reading fine, so you should be okay."

"Thanks for stopping by, Dustin," her dad said as he led the way back upstairs. "Appreciate it."

"Hey, happy to help," Mr. Negavi replied. "Dwayne's got a baseball game next week on Wednesday—maybe we'll see you there?"

"Definitely," Jules's dad promised, and she nodded as well. The two men shook hands, and Mr. Negavi waved good-bye to Jules before he stepped outside.

"That was kinda neat," Jules said after he'd left. She knew she'd be telling her class all about it tomorrow. She headed back up to her room. Time to get back to packing. Normally she just threw some sweats and some underwear into a gym bag, but she wanted to be a little more careful this time. After all, this wasn't just her staying over at her friend's house!

The entire freshman class at Albert Einstein Magnet High School ("Go Magnets!") was going to be spending the weekend sleeping over at the Natural History Museum—which could have wound up being really boring, she had to admit. Who wanted to sleep by a whole bunch of fossils or old arrowheads or bits of pottery?

Natural history is the study of organisms in their environment. This includes plants, animals, fungi, or any natural objects.

But she was still excited. Because, since this was a science trip, the students were being divided up into their science classes.

Which meant she'd be spending the whole weekend with Mr. Enright and the rest of STEM1!

Even though it was only the second month of school, Jules totally loved her science class. Mr. Enright was cool and funny, but also a little weird. And she liked all of her classmates, even Malik, who she'd never gotten along with at their middle school. But the best part was the way Mr. Enright made science interesting. Especially how he related it to real life. That's what STEM was all about, after all—

applying science, technology, engineering, and math to real-world problems.

Like last month, when they'd managed to help out during a flash flood. That had been awesome! Scary at times, but still awesome!

And Mr. Enright had promised that he'd have lots of nifty stuff for them to learn—and do—during this sleepover. So there was no way Jules was going to miss it.

Of course, there was always the risk of another blackout. But so what if the lights dimmed occasionally. It was annoying, sure, but that was about it. And she trusted her STEM teacher. Mr. Enright was always prepared for everything. She was sure he'd be ready in case the lights went out on them.

Now if she could just get ready herself—which meant figuring out which shirt to pack!

CHAPTER 2

CHECKING IN

"Sure you've got everything?" Malik Jamar's dad asked as they pulled up outside school and Malik hopped out.

"Should be good," Malik responded, doing a quick scan through the list in his head. Clothes, check. Toothbrush, toothpaste, dental floss, deodorant, brush, check. Phone and charger, check. Sleeping bag, blanket, and inflatable pillow, check. Backpack with regular schoolbooks, check. Money for lunch, and for vending machines at the museum if he needed a snack, check. "Yep, all set," he confirmed.

"Great. Have fun—and don't lose your phone," his dad warned with a half-serious look. "See you Sunday," he called as he drove off.

Malik groaned at that crack about the phone. Was he ever going to live that one down? He'd had to explain to his parents last month how he'd lost his phone during the flash flood, though he'd just said there'd been a sudden sinkhole and he'd tripped and dropped the phone down it. He'd left out the part where he'd been clowning around taking a selfie directly over the sinkhole—no reason to share that! Even so, his parents hadn't been thrilled about having to replace his phone so soon.

They'd eventually caved, though, when Malik had pointed out that without a phone he couldn't call them if he needed help. Or check in with them when he was out with friends. "It's for my own safety," he'd insisted, giving them his best puppy dog eyes. Which was why he now had the latest Encom smartphone, the Encom Unicator 3.

He wondered if Mr. Enright's Aunt Nancy had worked on it directly. I'll have to remember to ask him, Malik thought as he shouldered his backpack and sleeping bag and trudged down the walkway toward school—assuming he remembered amid all the other excitement.

He was looking forward to the weekend. Sleeping in a museum—how wild was that? And who knew what Mr. Enright would have them doing while they were there. Whatever it was, Malik was sure it'd be fun. Educational, too, but he was okay with that. He didn't mind learning new stuff—actually, he really liked it. As long as it wasn't boring.

And so far STEM class had never been boring!

"Yo, Malik," his friend Jay hollered from down the hall as Malik entered the school and headed for his locker. "How's it hanging?"

"It's all good, man," Malik called back without stopping. "You?"

"Yeah, all geared up to sleep with the fishes!" Jay answered with a grin.

"It's a museum, not an aquarium," Malik pointed out, laughing. "Any fishes there are gonna be nothing but old bones!"

"Good, then they won't keep me awake!" Jay replied. Several other kids were cracking up at the exchange, and Malik smiled. He had a feeling that conversation was going to get retold a few times today. That was cool.

Continuing on his way, exchanging nods and hellos and high fives with various other students, Malik rounded a corner—and nearly ran into Kevin Sumter, who was just emerging from a classroom.

"Hey, dude, whoa!" Malik said, backpedaling to avoid a collision. Then he had to adjust quickly, as the weight of his backpack and sleeping bag nearly made him wipe out anyway. "Head up, eyes forward, all right?"

Kevin glanced down at him—he was a tall, gangly kid, the kind you figured had to play basketball until you saw just how clumsy he was with regular stuff, never mind dribbling and shooting a ball. "Oh, sorry," he mumbled, extending a long-fingered hand to help Malik steady himself. "You okay?"

"Oh, yeah, fine." Malik brushed himself off even though he hadn't actually fallen. "What were you doing in there, anyway?" The classroom Kevin had stepped out of was an art room, Malik remembered. But Kevin didn't take art; he'd picked theater for his elective—Malik knew because they were in class together.

He was surprised to see the taller kid's face transform into a scowl. "They left the lights on," Kevin declared, glaring at the other students moving up and down the hall.

"Huh?" Malik glanced around but couldn't figure out who Kevin was referring to. "Who left what lights on?"

"Whoever used the art room last, they left the light on in there," Kevin answered. "Which means it was probably on all night. It drives me nuts when people do that." Wow, Malik thought, Kevin took turning off the lights really seriously!

"Uh, maybe the janitor turned it on this morning," Malik pointed out. "You know, right before school, so the classrooms'd all be ready when we got here? Pretty sure he goes around at night checking to make sure each room's closed up tight anyway, so wouldn't he have turned off the light then if it'd been left on?"

"Oh." He watched his classmate consider this. "Oh, yeah. You're right." The other boy actually looked relieved at being proven wrong, which Malik didn't really get, but whatever. "Thanks," Kevin told him. "I thought somebody'd been wasting electricity."

Now Malik was confused again. "How can you waste electricity?" he wondered aloud. "I mean, there's a limitless supply, right? Every time you flip the switch, there it is—it's not like we run out!"

Kevin stared down at him like he'd gone nuts. "Seriously, dude?" he asked. "Do you have any idea how much damage you could do with an attitude like that? Wow. You need to straighten that out, ASAP." And with that, shaking his head, Kevin walked away down the hall.

"I need to get my attitude straightened out?" Malik muttered after him, staring as the taller boy shouldered his way through the crowds. "I don't think I'm the one who's a weirdo around here, dude. Wow is right."

But whatever. Kevin was an oddball, but it wasn't Malik's problem. He adjusted his grip on his backpack and sleeping bag and resumed the trek toward his locker. That strange little encounter had cost him a few minutes, so he'd have to hustle if he wanted to drop off some of his things before heading to homeroom. And there was no way he wanted to be carrying all of this around all day!

As he walked, though, Malik's irritation at Kevin's odd behavior faded, to be replaced again by his general excitement about the upcoming trip. This was going to be a blast!

And since it was STEM and not theater, he wouldn't have to worry about dealing with Kevin and his bizarre notions all night. That was a relief!

CHAPTER 3

MAKING ROOM

"All right then, class," Mr. Enright announced as a bell rang somewhere overhead and echoed through their classroom's built-in speakers. "That's that for the day. Which means it's time to gather our gear and prepare for our trip!" He levered his tall, lanky frame off the stool he'd been perched on and gathered up a large hiking backpack that had been resting on the floor beside him. "Everyone set?"

Jules hopped down and grabbed her duffel bag and her sleeping bag, causing a slight twinge in her still-healing hands and wrists. "Set," she called out while her classmates all scrambled to collect their own things.

"Gear up and fall in!" Randall Warner, their teacher's aide, bellowed. As always, he was decked out like he was about to embark on a top-secret military mission—in a black T-shirt and black pants, with black boots and a black cap to finish the picture. His bag was already on his shoulders and looked like a more martial version of the backpack their teacher was sporting.

"Yeah, yeah," Malik muttered, collecting his belongings. "It's not like there's a race, is there? I mean, pretty sure the museum'll still be there if we're a few minutes late."

"Normally, I'd agree with you," Mr. Enright declared, shaking his head as he consulted a handsome wristwatch. "In this case, however, time is in fact of the essence. As this trip is a school-wide outing, rather than a more informal study session like the one we embarked upon last month, we will all be piling onto a handful of the school district's aging yellow buses. That means we must adhere to Dr. Pillai's schedule rather than our own, and thus we cannot afford to be late." Their teacher's strong British accent gave his instructions a pleasant lilt, but the message still came across loud and clear—hurry up!

"What about Bud?" Jules's classmate Tracey DeGuerra asked as they all headed toward the classroom door. "Isn't he coming?" Bud had been perched on the desk beside Mr. Enright all through class, getting up once or twice to clamber around the room by swinging from light fixture to light fixture, but that wasn't particularly strange.

After all, Bud was a monkey. A chimpanzee, to be precise, formerly an astronaut with NASA and now sort of a class mascot and unofficial second assistant. He was amazing, and all of them thought he was great, especially Malik—he and Bud hadn't gotten along at first, but they had patched things up and now were like best friends.

Right now Bud was standing on the desk waving good-bye, the way he often did at the end of class. Jules didn't know where the chimp went after class each day, but he rarely accompanied them when they left.

"Sadly, Bud will not be joining us," Mr. Enright replied, leading the way out into the hall and down it to the small elevator waiting there. "Though Dr. Pillai has agreed to let Bud assist with our class, she would prefer that he not interact with the student body as a whole."

"In other words," another classmate, Christopher Wong, offered, "she doesn't want everyone else at school to know we've got a chimp hidden down here." Chris was a musician and usually wore all black, so Jules was amused to see that instead of his usual black leather shoulder bag, he was carrying a bright pink backpack and a bright orange sleeping bag with hot pink butterflies on it. "They're my little sister's," Chris had explained, blushing, when he'd caught Jules staring at the gear earlier. "For Girl Scouts. I don't have a sleeping bag or a big enough backpack, so I had to borrow hers." Jules had nodded and done her best not to laugh.

Mr. Enright wasn't laughing right now, however, when he agreed with Chris's guess. "I do believe you are correct, Chris," their teacher said instead. "I do not know whether she is concerned about health issues or possible lawsuits, or just that every other student will clamor to be allowed to spend time with Bud, but whatever the reason, she has requested that he not accompany us on school-wide events. And I can see no reason to dispute her wishes on this." He smiled. "Not to worry, though; I am sure Bud will be waiting for us when we return on Monday."

The elevator doors slid open and they all piled in, Ilyana Desoff hitting the "S" button for "Surface" once they were all inside. A few seconds later the elevator pinged, then opened again, and they tumbled out into the gleaming elevator lobby then spilled out into the dingy old classroom beyond that. Jules couldn't help turning around to glance over her shoulder as they exited the classroom. As usual, the hologram there made it look like the room ended in an old, battered chalkboard mounted across the far wall. Only the class and probably Dr. Pillai knew what lay behind that image.

Speaking of their principal, she was waiting when Mr. Enright led the class down the main hall and out the front doors to the crowd waiting outside. "We have a small problem," Dr. Pillai declared once she'd spotted Mr. Enright and his class. "We don't have enough room on the buses for everyone."

"Oh?" Jules thought their small, sharply dressed principal was terrifying, but Mr. Enright never appeared to be too fazed. "How did that happen?" he asked now, raising one eyebrow to show his surprise.

"We have roughly one hundred and forty freshmen, plus five teachers and myself," Dr. Pillai answered. "Each school bus holds approximately fifty students. I requested three buses."

Mr. Enright turned to his class. "Where did our good principal go wrong?" he asked them.

Jules and her classmates immediately gathered in a small circle to confer. "Three buses at fifty people apiece should be one hundred and fifty, and we've only got one hundred and forty-five," Malik pointed out, "so it wasn't her math."

"The buses could fit fewer people than she thought," Ilyana offered. "That would mean we couldn't fit everyone." She tossed her long, pale blond hair back over her shoulder.

"She might be working from old numbers," Chris suggested, "and we've actually got more students than she realized."

"Maybe it's a weight issue," Tracey suggested.

She shifted the heavy-looking army rucksack she had slung over one shoulder. "Each bus can only handle so much weight, but with these bags we could be over the limit."

But Jules had another idea, one that Tracey had made her think of. "Maybe it's not about the weight at all," she said slowly. "Maybe it's about the volume."

Volume is the amount of space an object or substance occupies.

Mr. Enright had been listening in, and now he nodded. "All excellent guesses," he told them with a smile. "But I believe Jules had the correct answer. Unless I'm mistaken, Dr. Pillai based her request for buses upon the number of students going on this trip, but she failed to account for everyone's bags and backpacks and sleeping bags." He glanced over at the principal, who nodded sharply. "As a result," their teacher continued, "we do not have enough room to accommodate both students and supplies. Or do we?"

"Uh oh," Malik joked. "I feel a lesson coming on!" But he was grinning when he said it, and Jules knew he enjoyed these little problems as much as the rest of them.

"Okay," Tracey said, taking the lead, "let's do this. We've got three school buses, right? And just about a hundred and fifty students. That's fifty students per bus. But how much can each bus hold, really?"

Malik had already whipped out his phone and was typing in queries. "Looks like the standard school bus is nine and a half feet high, eight feet wide, and twenty-five feet long. They fit fifty-four students each, so fifty's not a problem."

Chris was nodding, tapping his fingers against his leg as he did the math. "So if we figure we're losing maybe five feet up front for the engine," he suggested, "that gives us, what, twenty by eight by nine and a half? That's fifteen hundred and twenty cubic feet."

"Sure, but how much space do the seats take up?" Ilyana asked. "And there's the aisles—we can't put anything in them; they have to keep those clear for safety reasons, right? Plus, those're the outside dimensions, not the inside ones."

"She's right," Tracey agreed. "You're gonna lose maybe six inches all around from the frame and the body." She was their resident gearhead, expert on all things automotive, so the rest of them knew not to argue with her on that one.

"So we're looking at more like nineteen and a half by seven and a half by nine?" Malik asked. He elbowed Chris. "How much's that, Mr. Calculator?" He was already tapping the numbers into his phone, but Chris beat him to the punch.

"One thousand, three hundred, and sixteen," Chris answered proudly. "And a quarter." He shrugged. "I'm good with numbers."

"Yeah, you are!" Malik agreed. Jules was impressed that he didn't seem at all put out at having been beaten. "Okay, so we've got about thirteen hundred cubic feet. How much do we lose to the seats? There's, what, nine rows on each side, eighteen seats in all?"

"Yep," Tracey confirmed, glancing inside the nearest bus. "And each seat's about three feet wide, two feet deep, and maybe three feet high at the seat. That's eighteen cubic feet each, times eighteen, which is . . ." She trailed off, and they all turned to Chris.

He laughed. "Three twenty-four," he answered. "That's an easy one!"

"So we've still got almost a thousand cubic feet left," Ilyana pointed out. "How much space does a regular student take up? Five to six feet tall, two feet wide, two feet deep? That's a maximum of twenty-four feet, and fifty students would equal one thousand, two hundred, and fifty—you're not the only one good at math!" She frowned. "But wait, that doesn't make any sense! That's more than we have left, and we know they fit! What'm I missing?"

Jules thought about it. All the math sounded right to her, but Ilyana was correct—they knew the bus would hold fifty students without a problem, even if the math claimed otherwise. So something didn't add up. She frowned and cupped one hand in the other, massaging her knuckles, which were still a bit sore.

But then she glanced down at what she was doing and almost shouted. "Got it!" she blurted out, holding up her hands. "We're looking at this wrong! We can't count the seats and the students separately, because once everyone's sitting down they take up the same space as the seats! They're overlapping, sharing the space!"

"Oh yeah, nailed it!" Tracey held up a hand for a high-five, and Jules obliged despite her sore fingers. "Students on seats—and hey, bags on students! I bet they tried piling their stuff on empty seats and then didn't have enough space left to fit everyone, when what they should've done—"

"—is sit down first and hold their stuff on their laps!" Malik finished for her. He gave Tracey an apologetic grin for cutting her off, but even though she shook her fist at him she was smiling too. "Nice one!"

They all turned to Mr. Enright, who was also smiling. "Well done!" he commended them. "I believe you've solved our little logistics issue!" He looked over at Dr. Pillai, who had also been listening in. "Shall we attempt the new arrangement, Madame Principal?" he asked her.

She nodded. "Yes." Then turned to give instructions to the vice principals and other teachers assisting in the process. "Everyone on the bus, carry your bags with you, hold them on your lap once you're seated."

"Actually," Ilyana offered, but so quietly only the rest of the class heard her, "if we've got nine rows, and we can fit six per row, we only need eight and a half, so one bench in the back could be used to pile up sleeping bags or something. That'd make it easier to carry the rest of our stuff ourselves, and we'd still have enough space to seat everybody."

"Good idea," Jules agreed, and she turned to tell Mr. Enright, who then relayed that to Dr. Pillai, who amended her instructions. Ilyana gave Jules a grateful smile as they filed onto their own bus—though she was perfectly talkative with the rest of their class, Ilyana could be a little shy around people she didn't know, and around most adults except for Mr. Enright.

The plan worked perfectly, and soon they were all seated and ready to go. "Another problem solved thanks to STEM," Mr. Enright announced, and Jules and her classmates cheered and clapped. "Now, onward to the museum!"

They continued laughing and hollering and whistling as the bus pulled away from the school. Their class trip was officially underway!

CHAPTER 4

GOING DARK

"Good afternoon, students!" the woman standing on the front steps of the museum called out as everyone piled off the buses. "My name is Ms. Dancy, and I'm the museum curator, which I guess makes me your host for the weekend!" Ms. Dancy was tall and had long blond hair pulled back in a very sensible braid. She was wearing a rather smart red suit, and Malik thought she looked more like a business executive than someone who ran a museum. Weren't museum employees supposed to be mousy little people who were more comfortable with exhibits than with people?

A **curator** is the person who maintains or runs a museum and is responsible for taking care of its collections.

Dr. Pillai must have shoved past the kids on her bus, or maybe she'd claimed the front seat right behind the bus driver, because she was already climbing the steps toward Ms. Dancy. "Ms. Dancy," she said, offering her hand to the curator. It was a funny image, just because their principal was so short and the museum curator was so tall.

"Lovely to see you again, Dr. Pillai," Malik heard Ms. Dancy say. "I've got everything all set up for you and your students."

"Excellent, thank you." The principal turned back toward the students and raised her voice. "Listen up! I want you to stay in your class groups and proceed inside in an orderly fashion! You're responsible for your own belongings, so make sure you have everything off the bus. Teachers, you already have your room assignments—please take your class there right away and get settled. I will be visiting each of you, along with Ms. Dancy, to make sure everything's all right." Then she swiveled back around and followed the curator into the museum.

"Was your principal ever in the military?" Randall asked quietly as they gathered around Mr. Enright and waited their turn to head in. "Because she'd make one heck of a squad commander!"

"Ha, yes, well, running a school is much like managing a military unit," Mr. Enright replied easily. "The biggest difference is that you can only hand out detentions and suspensions in school, and your students aren't armed. Usually." His voice drifted off and he looked like he was lost in a memory, which happened a lot. Not for the first time Malik wondered what their teacher's real story was. He certainly seemed to have led an interesting life so far—one a lot more exciting than one would expect from a science teacher!

Malik saw Jay and some other friends standing by the next bus over. "Hey, Malik!" Jay called out. "Watch out for the dinosaurs, yeah? I hear they get hungry at night!"

"Ha, sure—and you watch out for mummies," Malik replied. "Never know when they're gonna go after your scrolls!"

A **mummy** is an ancient Egyptian noble who, upon death, was subjected to mummification, a process in which the body was preserved within special wrappings inside a coffin-like sarcophagus. Mummies often appear in monster movies, rising from their tombs to wander the night still wearing their wrappings.

Laughter erupted around them, and several other kids joined in, making cracks that referred to the well-known movies and books about what happened after dark in certain famous museums. Malik saw Jules shake her head—she was always so serious!—but she was hiding a smile as she did. Ha! Even she thought it was funny!

Malik and his classmates were the third class to enter, and they stubbornly resisted Randall's shouts to march in step with one another. STEM1 was the smallest of the science classes, with only five of them, so they had a much easier time sticking together than any of the other four classes, and Mr. Enright smartly sidestepped the two classes ahead of them as soon as they were inside, leading his class off down a side corridor. "This way," he called over his shoulder, his long strides eating up the distance. Jules was able to keep up without a problem, as were Randall and Chris, but the rest of them had to break into a half-run to avoid being left behind.

"What's the hurry?" Malik muttered as he ran. "We're here all weekend!"

He caught glimpses of a few other rooms as they charged past and brief images of the exhibits they contained. One had what looked like tall, heavy wooden totem poles, another was filled with dioramas of animals in their native habitats, and a third looked like it had all sorts of fish—presumably also stuffed, or maybe just models—in their native waters. Maybe Jay would get to sleep with the fishes after all!

A **diorama** is a three-dimensional display in which figures are set up as if they were alive in their natural setting.

Finally, they reached a room that looked darker than the others. It was an interior room, so it didn't have any windows, but even so, Malik had expected it to be more brightly lit. "What's with the lights?" he asked as he followed the rest inside. For a brief second he wondered if Kevin had been wandering around turning them all off, but that didn't make any sense—they'd all arrived at the museum together.

"This room is kept dark on purpose," Mr. Enright answered, dropping his bags in one corner of the room and gesturing at the display cases all around them. Now Malik saw that most of those were dark as well—but several of them had some kind of glow deep within. "This room is dedicated to photosynthesis, bioluminescence, and other light-related science," their teacher continued. He grinned at them. "I thought it would make the perfect lesson for the weekend, considering the recent power outages we've all been experiencing."

Photosynthesis is the process by which a plant converts sunlight to chemical energy, which can then be used for food and other purposes. **Bioluminescence** is the production of light by a living organism.

"Bioluminescence?" Ilyana asked. "You mean like glowing fish? Sweet!"

"Quite right," their teacher answered. He was about to say more, but the sound of approaching footsteps cut him off. A second later, Ms. Dancy entered the room, followed closely by Dr. Pillai.

"Ah, you must be Mr. Enright!" Ms. Dancy said enthusiastically, shaking Mr. Enright's hand. "I've heard so much about you and your students! Wonderful stuff! And you were all so amazing during that flash flood last month—you're all real heroes!"

"Oh, well, thank you very much," Mr. Enright replied, and Malik thought his teacher looked a bit flushed. And was he stuttering? "That's most kind of you. We merely did what we could to help those in need, and of course to learn about the science behind it all in the process."

Behind them, Malik saw that Dr. Pillai was clenching her jaw. She'd been furious when she'd found out that Mr. Enright had taken them to the flood plain and potentially put the entire class at risk—and during the first week of school too! But it had all worked out okay, and all the attention the school had received afterward—most of it super-positive for helping the community and so on—had helped their principal get over it. For the most part.

"You've picked a really interesting exhibit for your home base," Ms. Dancy said, turning to the rest of them. "It's actually one of my favorite rooms, and I hope you really enjoy it. Plus," she added, "it's like you've got built-in nightlights!"

Dr. Pillai was no-nonsense and to the point, as usual. "Everything satisfactory here, Mr. Enright?" she asked.

"Oh, tip-top, madam," he replied with a short bow that drew a giggle from Ilyana and Jules—and, surprisingly, from Ms. Dancy as well! "All students present and accounted for, all properly equipped for the weekend, and the room is perfectly suited to our needs."

"Fine, we'll leave you to it for now," the principal told him. She checked her watch. "We'll have dinner at six, which is two hours from now. We'll announce it over the museum's intercom once it's ready, and then each class will assemble in the café."

"We will be there," Mr. Enright assured her.

"Let me know if you need anything else," Ms. Dancy added as she turned to follow Dr. Pillai out. "And have fun!"

"She seems nice," Ilyana commented once the two women had left.

Malik agreed, though he still thought the curator was too outgoing to be working in a museum.

"Yes, very pleasant," Mr. Enright agreed. "And very good at her job as well—this museum is one of the best in the country for natural history, eclipsed only by some of the more famous locales like the Natural History Museum in New York or the Smithsonian in D.C." Malik nudged Chris, who grinned back. Those were the same two featured in all those movies!

"Where should we put our stuff?" Tracey asked. Like the rest of them, she was still wearing her backpack and had her sleeping bag and clothing bag slung at her feet.

"Oh, anywhere around the room ought to do," their teacher replied. "For now, let's set them all against the far wall so they aren't in our way. We can arrange things more to our liking after dinner, but there's no sense in having to step over sleeping bags in the meantime, right? Did enough of that on that dig in Cairo; not keen to repeat it." There it was again, Malik thought—another brief hint at Mr. Enright's former life, offered in passing and never explained. The man was a mystery!

Malik added his bags to the pile, and then they all gathered around Mr. Enright again near the center of the room. It wasn't as big as some of the other exhibit rooms they'd passed by, but considering there were only seven of them, he thought they'd have plenty of space.

"Now," their teacher began, "as I was saying before, this room is dedicated to light and light-based science. I thought it was particularly appropriate for us, given current events. It's a fascinating field, and—"

Yet again he was cut off, but this time not by footsteps. Instead, Mr. Enright stopped because the room had suddenly gone dark. Completely pitch-black dark, like someone had poured black paint over all of them. It was so dark that at first Malik thought there was something wrong with his eyes, but he blinked hard, seeing flashes as his lids pressed shut tight, and it was still utterly black around him. He couldn't even make out Chris or Ilyana or the others, and they were standing right next to him!

"What just happened?" Tracey called out, and Malik could hear an edge of panic in her voice. "Why's it so dark?" Was tough, street-smart Tracey afraid of the dark? Malik wondered.

"I'll tell you why," Jules answered, and she sounded concerned but still calm. Which wasn't a surprise—Malik had seen enough of her games to know that his classmate could keep her cool under pressure. "It's a blackout!"

CHAPTER 5

FEELING THE WAY

The first person to respond to Jules's statement, surprisingly, was Randall. "Superlative!" Their teacher's aide declared. "The perfect time for stealth ops!" It was so dark that Jules couldn't even see him, but she could still picture the gleam in his eye as he rubbed his hands together. Randall was a little odd.

"Wow, this sucks," Chris commented. "Talk about crappy timing—and us in a room without windows!" His voice was coming from somewhere to the side, and Jules tried to remember where he'd been standing when the lights had gone out. Malik was next to her, she thought, and Chris was next to him, right? Yes, that sounded about right. And Tracey was on her other side, with Ilyana past her, and Mr. Enright and Randall beyond her. That was all of them.

There was a loud clatter, and then a muffled crash, and an "oof!" "Sorry, sorry," Chris declared. "Tripped over my bag—at least, I think it was my bag!"

"Nobody move!" Tracey shouted. Jules thought her friend sounded a little alarmed. "We could run right into each other—or into the exhibits! And they're glass!"

Jules thought that seemed a bit unlikely—the exhibits had been several feet away, as she recalled—but didn't say that. It was clear that Tracey didn't like the dark much. Jules wasn't too thrilled about not being able to see, either, but at least they weren't moving, or surrounded by sharp objects, or anything like that. They were all together in the middle of a room. She could handle that. Though when they did need to go anywhere—like the bathroom—that might get tricky.

She heard another thump, though this one sounded a bit different, sort of meatier. "Found the wall," Randall declared, his voice farther away than it had been before. "It's right over here, next to my head."

"Good job," Malik called out. "Now stay there so if we need the door we'll bump into you first instead of it—that'll be a lot softer." Jules laughed, as did several of the other students. Leave it to Malik to find the humor in the situation!

"Nobody's going to bump into anything," Mr. Enright assured all of them, his voice perfectly calm. "Everyone just relax. We're going to be just fine."

"How can you be sure?" Tracey demanded. "What if somebody trips over something sharp and we can't see to help them? What if somebody sneaks in here and hurts someone while nobody can see? What if Randall actually bumped into something big and heavy and glass and it's falling over right now and we don't know it? We could be about to get hit by glass shards, and we won't see them coming!"

Jules reached out and rested her hand on what she thought was Tracey's arm. "Hey, it's okay," she promised. "We're all right here."

"Yeah, and I left all my sharp objects in my other bag," Malik joked. "So it's all good."

"Here's what I want everyone to do," their teacher told them. "First, I want all of you to sit down just where you are. Feel around you with your hands and feet in case your bags are there, and just shove them in front of you or behind you, but don't actually move around yourself. Okay?"

There was a lot of shuffling. Jules knew her bag was right at her feet, so she nudged it forward a little and then dropped into a cross-legged position. All around her she could tell that her classmates were doing the same thing. There were a few grunts and groans, and one "hey, watch it!" from Chris, followed by a "sorry, dude" from Malik, but after a minute or two they all went quiet again.

It was strange how, without light, your other senses ran wild. The museum had tall ceilings, Jules had noticed when they'd come in, high enough that the very tops had already been shrouded in shadow even with the lights on. But now, sitting on the floor in the dark, it felt like she was in some sort of immense, nearly endless cave, with no hint of wall or ceiling anywhere around. She felt a little dizzy at the thought, actually, and placed both her hands flat on the floor to either side of her. That helped—the contact with the cold, smooth marble reassuring her that she wasn't just floating in empty space somehow.

The other thing that helped ground her was Mr. Enright's voice. "Everyone settled?" he asked, which elicited a wave of replies. "Good. Now close your eyes."

"Why?" Ilyana asked. "It's already dark!"

"Trust me," he answered. "Close your eyes, and keep them closed until I say otherwise. Ready? Close them now!"

Jules obediently squeezed her eyes shut. Ilyana was right; it didn't make any difference to her in terms of what she could see or sense, but she trusted Mr. Enright. She automatically started counting in her head once she'd closed her eyes, and she'd just reached thirty when he called out, "Right, open your eyes."

She did—and gasped. "Hey, I can see!" she announced.

"Yeah, me too!" Tracey declared beside her, her relief obvious. "Well, sort of."

"Sort of" was accurate, Jules realized. She couldn't really see, not fully, but she could make out a little, which was a lot more than she'd been able to do a minute before. Tracey was now a dark shape beside her, and she could see the rest of her class as well, though not any features. She could also make out the door, which was a big patch of shadow just a few degrees lighter than the rest of their surroundings.

"Closing your eyes gave them a chance to adjust," Mr. Enright explained, every moment a potential teaching lesson. "Your pupils dilated, which means they are now allowing in the maximum amount of light possible. It's rare to find complete darkness unless you've taken steps to deliberately block off all light, so we're now seeing shadows rather than total darkness, but nothing's actually changed. Just our perceptions."

A **pupil** is the black circle in the center of your eye. The colorful part surrounding it is the iris. The pupil expands or contracts to allow light through to the retina.
Dilate means to become wider, larger, or more open.
Contract means to become smaller.

"That's a pretty cool trick," Chris commented. "Does it only work in the dark? I mean, can you deliberately adjust your pupils to deal with more light too?"

"You can," their teacher answered—Jules could see him well enough to tell that he was leaning back, hands out to either side. "If you were to stare at a bright light for a second, your pupils would contract to protect your optic nerves from getting too much light at once. Then you'd be able to see in bright light without having to squint as much, because your pupils would stay contracted for a few minutes."

"If you did that and the lights went out, though, you'd really be blind, right?" Malik asked. "Because your eyes would adjust to bright light and then have an even harder time with the dark?"

"Absolutely," Mr. Enright agreed. "You'd have to close them and let them slowly dilate again, the way we just did, but for a bit longer to make sure they'd dilated fully. That's why, in a situation like this when you're moving around in the dark, you actually want to avoid bright lights—if you were to see a bright light right now it'd hurt because your pupils are so fully dilated, and then you'd have a much harder time getting your eyes to adjust back to the dark again."

"I've seen that in movies," Ilyana offered. She was their resident book and movie expert. "Where the hero blinds the bad guys by shining a light in their eyes or setting off a flare or a camera flash while they're in the dark."

"Flashbangs," Randall declared. When everyone turned to look at him—or squint at the dark shape that they thought was him—he shrugged. "That's what the military calls stun grenades. They make a really loud bang and a really bright flash of light. Leaves people blind and stunned for a few seconds, which is enough to get the drop on them. Works best if it's dark, so your pupils are already dilated."

Jules had been glancing around them while they talked, trying to figure out just how far she could see in the dim lighting. "Hey," she asked now, "what're those blobs over there?" She waved her hand toward the far wall, and what looked like very faint squiggles of light at what would have been chest height if she'd been standing up.

"Ah, good eye," Mr. Enright complimented. "Those are the bioluminescent specimens. Normally you can't see them well, even though this room is kept dim, but now they're showing up nicely. Let's go have a look, shall we? Everyone stand up, slowly, and reach out to put your hand on the shoulder of the person to your right. Ilyana, you wait there while I step closer and take the lead. Randall, can you rejoin us and follow Chris?"

"On it," Randall replied at once, and tromped back over. Apparently his eyes had also adjusted, because he didn't trip on anything or kick anyone as he made his way to the back of their little line.

"Everyone ready?" Mr. Enright called out a moment later. Jules nodded, her hand on Tracey's shoulder and Malik's on hers, before realizing that their teacher wouldn't actually be able to see that subtle motion. "Yes!" she called out instead, in ragged chorus with the rest. "Right," he responded. "Let's go, then. Roughly ten paces, straight ahead, normal walking pace. Follow me!"

It was very strange to walk without really being able to see where you were going. Jules was glad Tracey was in front of her, and she concentrated on keeping a few feet of distance between them so she didn't trip over her friend. Time was also hard to judge in the dark, it turned out, because it felt like they'd been walking for at least ten minutes before she finally heard her teacher order them to stop, but she knew the room wasn't really that big. How weird that sight played such a big part in interpreting so many things!

"Here we are," Mr. Enright told them. "We're right by the exhibit cases now. Can you see them?"

"Yes," Jules and the others responded. This close, she could actually make out a faint sheen that had to be the glass. And within that was a tiny glowing thing that, after a second, she realized was some sort of tiny fish. "Oh!" she studied it more closely. "Wow, it's like it's glowing!"

"It *is* glowing," their teacher corrected gently. "It's producing its own light from within. That's how bioluminescence works—it's a chemical process that takes place inside the creature's body, mixing chemicals together to produce its own light."

"Like one of those glow sticks," Malik piped up. "They work that way too, right?"

"They do indeed," Mr. Enright confirmed. "That's chemiluminescence, or light caused by a chemical reaction, the same as the bioluminescence in these creatures."

"Why're they all fish and stuff?" Tracey asked. "I thought there were lizards and bugs that glowed too."

"There are some," their teacher replied. "Not as many, though. And most of them are larva rather than full-formed insects, which means the museum would have to replace them constantly. The firefly is one of the only insects that's bioluminescent as an adult."

"Too bad we don't have a whole bunch of fireflies," Jules thought aloud. "We could portion them out into jars, arrange them around the room, and it'd be like lighting the place with lanterns—but natural ones."

Mr. Enright nodded. "People have been catching fireflies and putting them in jars or other containers for centuries," he agreed. "It's very likely that they were one of the first portable light sources, precisely as you suggested. And as long as you leave air holes, and line the bottom of the container with some fresh leaves, those little bugs can last for a while—and continue to provide light each and every night."

"I'd settle for the modern equivalent," Tracey groused. "Like, a few of those glow sticks Malik was talking about."

"I do have one in my backpack," their teacher admitted. "But it would not be a terribly good idea to break it out. It only provides a limited amount of light, and as I mentioned before, it would ruin what little night sight you've started to attain. Better to use whatever ambient light we have and make do."

What he said made sense, but Jules still couldn't help wishing for a whole bunch of glow sticks, like Tracey had said. Or jar upon jar of fireflies. Or just a bunch of big, powerful flashlights. Or something! Her eyes had adapted a little now, enough that she could make out her friends and, if she really squinted, just about see their faces. But it was still really creepy sitting here in the dark!

CHAPTER 6

POWERING DOWN

"I'm getting really tired of these blackouts," Chris muttered as they sat there. They'd just eaten a sort of dinner, if you could call it that—Mr. Enright had passed out cereal bars and juice boxes, so at least they weren't starving, but it was a far cry from a real meal as far as Malik was concerned.

"I hear you, man," Malik agreed. "Seriously lame."

"Perhaps now is a good time to talk about that," Mr. Enright suggested. Malik could just make him out in the darkness. "For example, what is the biggest problem when there's a blackout? What is it you miss the most?"

"No Internet!" Malik answered at once. That drew chuckles from around the room.

Even their teacher laughed. "True," he agreed, "and I, for one, am very sad when I don't have streaming video and wind up missing *NCIS*. But what's the biggest problem, rather than the biggest annoyance?"

For a second, no one responded. Malik wracked his brain for an answer, and he was sure his classmates were doing the same. What was the biggest problem when there was a blackout? No electricity? Well, duh, but that was too general, he was sure. And that was really the cause, not the result. So what is it they lose when they don't have power? Lights? Obviously, and annoying but not really a problem—they were managing without lights just fine for now. What else? What else got turned off when the power died?

It was Ilyana who came up with it first. "No refrigeration!" she all but shouted. "If the power's out, so's your fridge and your freezer, and everything in them can spoil!"

"Very good," Mr. Enright complimented. "You're right; that's a real problem. What can we do about it? Obviously we can't get the power back on, which means we can't restore the refrigeration, but can we preserve the food somehow?"

"You can transfer all the food into coolers," Malik offered. "Use freezer packs and ice and stuff. That'll keep 'em cool, at least for a while, and it doesn't use electricity."

"Excellent suggestion," their teacher said. "Years ago, before it was common for every house to have electricity, instead of a refrigerator and freezer people had what was called an icebox. Ever heard of one?"

Refrigeration is keeping an item or items at a set temperature, usually well below room temperature, by storing them within a structure designed to cool them.

A **freezer pack** is a portable object filled with water or some other liquid. The pack is placed in the freezer, where the liquid freezes. Then the freezer pack can be placed in a cooler in order to keep the rest of the cooler's contents cold.

"Isn't that another name for a freezer?" Ilyana asked. "I'm sure I heard it in a movie once."

"It is now," Mr. Enright answered, "but originally the icebox was exactly that—a big box that held a huge slab of ice, and then you stored your food in there with the ice to keep everything cold. Ice deliverymen would drive around in ice trucks, bringing fresh ice to each house when the old one melted. It didn't work as well as our fridges and freezers do now, but it was a lot better than nothing—and the iceboxes themselves didn't need any kind of power at all. Just ice."

"That's kind of neat," Chris said, and Malik nodded before he realized nobody could see the gesture.

"My mom's always yelling at my little brother to stop standing with the fridge door open all the time," Tracey volunteered, "because she says we're letting all the cold air out. So, if you keep the doors shut, does that really help hold it in longer?"

"It does," their teacher replied. "Most definitely. Fridges and freezers are heavily insulated to keep the cold in, and the longer you leave them shut, the longer they can do that. They'll eventually warm regardless, of course, but you can delay it a bit. If the power goes out, it's best to take out a few things to cook or eat right away, things that are most likely to spoil first, and then close the door and don't open it again until you must."

"Wait, how can you cook anything?" Jules asked. "Don't most stoves use electricity, too? We've got a gas stove at home, but I think it's still got electricity for something."

"For the ignition," Mr. Enright confirmed. "That's right. Also for the timer, the oven light, things of that nature. Some stoves even have a built-in safety feature so if the power goes out, the gas cuts off as well, because they're worried that without the electrical ignition the gas could somehow start to leak out on its own."

Malik knew the answer to this one, though. "You can still grill," he pointed out. "Even if you've got an electric grill, you can always put charcoal or wood in it and light it using a match, but lots of grills don't have any power at all, so they'll work fine. Same with campfires, if you're someplace where you can start one."

"Sure, but you can't light a campfire indoors," Jules responded. "You'd get smoke everywhere."

"Not just smoke, but carbon monoxide," their teacher added. "That's a natural byproduct of most fires, and outside it's fine, but indoors you could put yourself at serious risk. Malik is correct about grilling outdoors, however. And there are some small camp stoves designed to work indoors or out—they can fit over a single burner on your stove, or on a small plate on your table, and they run on a Sterno can, so they're small and safe and simple to use."

Carbon monoxide is an odorless, colorless gas. It forms when carbon is burned. Carbon monoxide is poisonous to most mammals and can be fatal if breathed in too much.
Sterno is a fuel made from jellied alcohol and packaged in small cans to serve as a portable heat source for cooking.

Malik hadn't heard of those camp stoves but made a mental note to check into them when he got home. That might be a fun thing to bring along on the next family camping trip.

"At least you'd still have water," Tracey said.

But Chris shot that down. "No, you wouldn't," he argued. "Think about it—our water's all from water plants and stuff, right? Those run on electricity too! Without power, those plants shut down, which means no new water being pumped out to all the houses. Or schools. Or museums."

"Very true," Mr. Enright agreed. "That's why it's always best to keep bottled water on hand. And if there's a blackout, don't use the sinks or toilets any more than necessary. Toilets have a tank, of course, and some water collects in the pipes, plus your home will have some in its hot water heater, but you don't want to risk running out when you need it, so it's best to conserve as much as possible."

Unfortunately, talking about not being able to go to the bathroom made Malik realize that he suddenly really needed to pee. He thought he heard squirming from some of the other kids as well, and it looked like most of them were also shifting around on the floor. So at least he wasn't the only one!

"Does that mean we can't use the bathroom?" Ilyana asked. "Or just that we shouldn't flush?" Which—ew!—but Malik agreed that she had a point.

"You shouldn't use it if you can avoid going," their teacher answered, "and although I know you may think it's gross, if you can get away with not flushing, that would be best as well. Sometimes, however, you simply need to use the facilities and hope for the best."

I can hold it, Malik decided, forcing himself to settle back down. At least for now.

"That's all cool info and such," Tracey was saying, "about what to do during a blackout. But what about stopping them altogether? Is there a way to do that?"

"Not any one surefire method," Mr. Enright replied, "much as I wish there were. But there are certainly ways to reduce the risk of having a blackout, as well as ways to prepare in case you do have one. Would you like to know what they are?"

"Yes!" Malik shouted back, along with all the others.

Even in the near-dark he could see their teacher's big, pleased smile. "Capital!" Mr. Enright announced, rubbing his hands together like a small child who's just been offered a huge lollipop or some other fancy treat. Then he laughed. "Alas, I cannot show them to you right this instant," he explained, sounding both disappointed and also amused. "Because, you see, there's no power just now." They all laughed. "But first thing in the morning, we'll go have a look-see. Right?"

"What'll we do until then?" Jules asked.

"Hmm, well, perhaps we should go around and check on the other classes," their teacher suggested. "I'm sure many of them are even more concerned than you are, and it might help to be reassured by classmates and friends."

"Nice," Malik agreed. "But don't you think it's gonna be a little hard for us to do that when we can't see where we're going? Because, y'know, blackout?"

"Indeed." Again, just from the tone of his voice,

Malik was sure their teacher was smiling. "I might be able to assist there. Hang on." He could just make out Mr. Enright grabbing one of his own bags, hauling it toward him, and then opening it and rummaging through it. "Let's see," Malik heard their teacher mutter. "Flashlight, batteries, hand-powered radio, solar charger—fat lot of good that'll do me tonight!— dried food, bottled water, blanket, first-aid kit . . . aha! Here they are!" He hauled something out of the bag—Malik couldn't see well enough to tell what—and began handing something around. When Malik got one, he thought at first it was a small octopus—lots of tentacles, kind of clingy—but then realized it was actually some sort of rubbery strap that attached to either side of a pair of short, stubby cylinders, each one about as wide around as a thick flashlight. The ends of the cylinders were smooth and hard, and Malik tapped one with his fingernail, producing a ringing sound. It was glass, which meant probably a lens of some sort.

It was obvious what their teacher wanted them to do with this, so Malik shrugged and pulled the whole thing over his head and down, adjusting the cylinders so that they were properly positioned over each eye, and gasped.

He could see again!

CHAPTER 7

SEEING THE LIGHT

"Wow!" Jules whispered as she looked around. "This is so wild!"

"Yeah," Tracey agreed next to her. "Wild—but awesome!"

Jules had to agree. She could see her friend clearly again, which was amazing. Admittedly, Tracey was a bright yellow-green, but so was everything else around them. The important thing was that she could see!

Her classmates were all pulling their own headsets on and looking around. Jules saw Ilyana glancing her way and waved. Her friend cheerfully waved back.

"These are wicked!" She heard Chris say. "They're night vision goggles, right?"

"That's right," Mr. Enright agreed. Jules could see him as clearly as the others, and like them, he was wearing goggles of his own. "To be precise, they're night optical/observation devices, or NODs. These are very similar to what the military uses on stealth missions."

"Yes!" Randall declared behind them, leaping to his feet. The goggles on his face made him look like a strange frog-man or something. "Stealth ops!"

"How do they work?" Tracey asked. Jules was glad to note that her friend had calmed down completely now. She was feeling a lot more relaxed herself. Being able to see again really helped!

"Good question," their teacher replied. "How do you *think* they work?"

"Are they infrared?" Ilyana asked. "I remember reading something about infrared lenses somewhere. But then everything'd be red, wouldn't it? I'm seeing all green instead. It's like you've all become plant people!" She giggled a little at the thought, and Jules discovered that it was really tough to roll your eyes when wearing goggles.

Infrared is electromagnetic radiation with a wavelength greater than that of visible red light but less than that of microwaves. Infrared is just beyond the visible end of the light spectrum.

"The first night vision scopes and goggles were infrared," Mr. Enright conceded. "That was back in World War II, when snipers used infrared beams to light up their targets—their scopes could make out the infrared, so they could see what they were shooting at, but the beams were invisible to the naked eye." He shook his head. "Those systems were really big and clunky, though, and they required a lot of power to operate, so they didn't work well for people trying to move quietly and slip in places."

"Isn't there something like a starlight scope?" Malik asked. Jules glanced over at him, as did a few of the others, and he shrugged. "I heard some guy talking about it once," he explained.

"There is, yes," Mr. Enright answered. "Those were the first passive night vision tools, which means instead of firing a beam out and then reabsorbing it to get data, they simply took in the available sensory data and magnified it. Starlight scopes first came out in the late 1970s. American forces relied heavily upon them during the Gulf War and the Iraq War." He tapped his goggles. "These are technically third-generation night vision goggles, or GEN-IIIs. They use what's called an image-intensifier tube—basically they take in ambient light and amplify it almost fifty thousand times. In order to do that, they use photocathodes, which are negatively charged electrodes coated with a photosensitive compound. They react to the light the same way the film does in a camera, converting light to an electron current, which is then processed through something called a microchannel plate to detect the particles and form them into a spatial image. They also have what's called an automatic gated power supply system, or an ATG. That regulates the voltage to the photocathode, which means these goggles can actually adjust to changing light conditions."

"So if the lights suddenly went on, we wouldn't be blinded?" Ilyana asked.

"Not as much as you might otherwise," the teacher answered. "A really bright light might still cause a flare, but a more subtle shift, like a battery-powered lantern, won't affect you at all."

"Why were you carrying a bunch of night vision goggles around in your bag?" Jules asked. "Did you know there'd be a blackout?" She knew their teacher liked to be prepared, but this seemed a bit thorough even for him!

He laughed. "No, though there was a good chance," he said. "Still, we were staying here overnight, and I'd wanted to talk about light and dark anyways, so I thought it'd be good fun to bring these along. Good thing I did!"

"Definitely," Malik agreed, waving his hands in front of his face and following their motion. "These are totally boss. Can we keep them?"

"Oh, of course," their teacher answered with another laugh. "Provided your parents are willing to shell out the ten thousand dollars or so that each set costs." Jules froze, as did her friends. She was afraid to move in case she somehow dropped or damaged the goggles she was wearing! Ten thousand dollars! That was like the price of a small car!

"These are the real deal," Mr. Enright continued. "They're military grade. That's why they're so pricey. A lot of times, when you see something advertised as night vision, it's really just a good flashlight or tinted lenses to filter the light and let you see a little better. Not like these."

Malik had another question. "Didn't I see a movie where they had night vision goggles with four lenses?" he asked. "What's up with that? It's not like they had four eyes!"

"Those were panoramic goggles," their teacher told him. "They work exactly the same as these, except that they offer a wider field of vision."

A **panorama** is an unobstructed, wide view in all directions.

"Great for stealth ops," Randall declared suddenly. He'd snuck up beside Malik and spoke right in his ear, making Malik jump. "Harder to sneak up on people if they can see to the side instead of just right in front," he added, laughing.

"Randall is correct," Mr. Enright confirmed. "Panoramic goggles allow you to see to the side without turning your head, which can be useful to avoid surprises." He startled them, then, by clapping his hands together and rising to his feet. "Everyone up, then!" he announced. "Time to take these goggles on the road!"

That sounded good to Jules. She had to admit, she'd been feeling a little claustrophobic stuck in their little exhibit room, at the same time as she'd felt like there weren't any walls or ceiling around her. Now that she could see, even if her vision was a little weird, she was eager to stretch her legs. And letting everybody else know everything was okay sounded like the perfect excuse, plus it would be a nice thing to do.

Claustrophobia is an irrational fear of enclosed spaces.

"Do we know what rooms everybody else is in?" Chris asked as they gathered near the door. "Should we split up or stay together?"

"I think pairs would be best," their teacher replied. "That way you're not alone, but we can still cover more ground than if we all went around together. I'm afraid I don't know which rooms the other four teachers are in, but I'm sure we'll find them as we wander. If nothing else, we should be able to hear them!"

Jules immediately tapped Tracey on the shoulder. "Partners?" she asked. Tracey was her closest friend in STEM class.

"Heck, yeah!" Tracey agreed with a grin. "Let's do this thing!"

Laughing, Jules followed her out into the hall. Behind her, she saw Chris and Malik pairing up. For a second she thought that would leave Ilyana with Randall and felt bad—their gung-ho teacher's aide could be a bit much sometimes—but then Mr. Enright stepped forward and suggested Malik go with Ilyana, while he and Chris walked around together. That was better.

Of course, that left Randall on his own, but he didn't seem too concerned. "Commencing stealth ops," he declared, saluting Mr. Enright before disappearing silently down the hall. Jules shook her head. That guy was weird!

"So, some school trip, huh?" Tracey asked as they walked. Their footsteps were loud on the marble floor, especially since they'd quickly outdistanced the others.

"Yeah," Jules agreed. "Still, it's kind of fun—at least now that we have these."

"I hear you. I don't mind saying that the dark was freaking me out a bit." Tracey shivered. "I'm so not a fan of being blind."

"Definitely. I—" Jules was interrupted as a dark figure suddenly leaped out at them from behind a display, shouting "BOO!"

"Aaah!" she and Tracey both screamed, backpedaling quickly. Glass display cases lined the walls here, and Jules bumped into one of them, hard enough to shake the whole case. Something within it toppled and made a loud clunking noise as it fell.

"Ha!" The shape turned out to be Randall. "Ambush successful!"

Jules shoved him hard enough to make him stumble. "Randall, you jerk! Look what you did!" she peered into the case. It was filled with trilobites and other small fossils. After a second she spotted the one she must have knocked over, which was a trilobite about the size of her palm. Fortunately, it didn't look like it was damaged at all. She let out a sigh of relief.

A **trilobite** is a small, extinct sea creature from the Paleozoic era. Trilobites were arthropods, which is the scientific family that also includes insects, spiders, and crabs.
A **fossil** is the remains of an ancient plant or animal, preserved in rock and stone.

"Relax," Randall told her, rubbing his shoulder where she'd pushed him. "It's a top priority to test our equipment to its fullest. That requires pitting ourselves against one another to study vulnerabilities, weak spots, and equipment limitations." He smirked. "Also, how high you jump when you get spooked."

Jules went to shove him again, but he backed away and then turned, took a few steps, and vanished. That was the thing about these goggles, Jules was starting to realize. They let her see really well, even in darkness, but only to a certain distance. Past that, it was all just one big blank.

"He must've gotten ahead of us somehow," Tracey said as they started walking again, a little more carefully this time. "I guess he's probably worn these things before, being ROTC and all, so he's more used to them. He probably heard us coming and huddled somewhere, just waiting for us. What a jerk."

"Seriously," Jules agreed. She was still seething. Having fun was all well and good, but not at somebody else's expense. And what if she'd really broken something? Or hurt herself? Randall obviously didn't care.

But he was going to, she promised herself. One way or another, she was going to make him sorry.

CHAPTER 8

ON THE CASE

"This is just like in all the movies!" Ilyana enthused as she and Malik explored one of the museum corridors together. "So cool!"

Even though he agreed, Malik still found himself laughing at his classmate's enthusiasm. He liked Ilyana just fine, so he hadn't minded when Mr. Enright had assigned them as partners. But she was *really* into her movies and books and shows!

It was killer, though, that they could see so clearly even though the corridor was still pitch black. He'd pulled his goggles up at one point, just to compare, and the difference had been startling. More than night and day, because usually at night you still had a little bit of light. This was total darkness versus being able to see perfectly fine, even if everything was green.

"Hey, hear that?" Malik asked her suddenly. They both froze like statues so their own footsteps wouldn't interfere. Sure enough, he heard it again. It sounded like—

"Voices!" Ilyana practically shouted in his ear. "We found one of the other classes!"

She raced down the hall toward the sounds, and Malik hurried after her. For somebody who often acted really shy around other people, and who usually had her nose buried in a book or her eyes glued to a screen, that girl had a lot of energy! And she could really run!

The only reason Malik was able to finally catch up to her at all was because she stopped to wait for him right outside the door to a large exhibit hall filled with glass display cases he couldn't see into clearly.

Right now, however, his and Ilyana's focus was on the thirty or so kids sitting on the floor and the teacher standing a short distance away from them, pacing anxiously. Malik recognized her after a second.

"It's Mrs. Cavanaugh," he told Ilyana. "I was in her class the first day, before I got moved to STEM. Hopefully she'll remember me."

"Go for it," Ilyana answered softly. "I've got your back." A huge grin ruined any attempt at her being serious and action-movie tough, and Malik snorted at her before entering the exhibit room and making his way to the teacher.

"Mrs. Cavanaugh!"

She swiveled around at the sound of her own name, clearly trying to act like the darkness didn't bother her. She actually had a flashlight in her hand, but oddly enough it wasn't on. Which was fine with Malik—if it had been, the light might've blinded him.

"It's Malik, Malik Jamar," he told her. "And my classmate, Ilyana Desoff. From STEM. Mr. Enright wanted us to go around and make sure everybody was okay."

"Oh, that's very thoughtful of you—and Mr. Enright," Mrs. Cavanaugh replied. Despite the darkness, she touched her hair like she was trying to make sure it looked okay, and beside Malik he heard Ilyana trying not to laugh. "Yes, yes, we're fine, thank you. A little disoriented, of course, but otherwise all right." She bit her lip. "Well, except for—" she paused.

Malik stepped a little closer and lowered his voice so the rest of the class wouldn't hear. "What's wrong? What happened? Is somebody hurt?"

"No, no, we're all fine," the science teacher repeated. She sighed. "Except that we're one student short."

"Who's missing?" Ilyana asked. She'd come closer to take part in the quiet conversation.

"Kevin Sumter. He was with us when we got off the bus," Mrs. Cavanaugh recalled, "because I took roll and we had everyone. The lights went out right after we got in here, then Dr. Pillai came by and said we'd continue the field trip because we were already here and it was going to be dark out soon anyway and we couldn't very well leave now when none of the streetlights or traffic lights were working. Then she left, and when I finally got everyone settled down enough to do a head count again, he was missing."

Malik shook his head. Twice in one day with Kevin? What were the odds?

"We'll find him," he promised Mrs. Cavanaugh. "Don't worry."

But Ilyana had a different question—the same one Malik had been dying to ask but hadn't. "You've got a flashlight," she said to the science teacher. "Why aren't you using it?"

Mrs. Cavanaugh smiled. "Most of us teachers thought to pack flashlights," she explained. "The only problem is, we each have only one or two of them—not enough to go around, certainly. And of course they have limited battery life. So I'm conserving energy. When someone needs to use the bathroom, I let them borrow the flashlight so they can find their way there and back. And when we're getting ready for bed I'll let small groups use it to go and get changed, after first walking around with it so everyone can dig through their bags and find what they need. But I can't just have it on all the time, or it could die on me right when we really need it.

That made a lot of sense. Malik remembered that Mr. Enright had listed a flashlight when he'd been digging through his own bag looking for the goggles, but their teacher hadn't even taken his out. Of course, he'd had something a whole lot better for them!

Just then, one of the students called out, "Malik, is that you?" It was his friend Cassie.

"Hey, Cass," he replied, walking over to her and tapping her on the shoulder as he bent down beside her. "You doing okay?"

"Sure, I love sitting around in the dark," she told him. "How about you? Why aren't you with your class?"

"Oh, our teacher asked us to check in on the other classes," Malik replied. "We've got these killer night vision goggles so we can actually find our way around and everything."

"Seriously? Can I see?" Cassie exclaimed. Malik hesitated, but only for a second. He and Cassie had been friends pretty much their whole lives. She was cool. So he pulled off the headgear and helped her put it on. It was weird being plunged back into the dark again—in some ways it wasn't as bad as the first time, because he knew it was there and what to expect, but in other ways it was worse, because he'd gotten used to being able to see despite the dark.

"This is sick!" Cassie declared, turning her head this way and that. "I can see everything!"

Of course everyone else in the class heard her and wanted to have a try. But Malik didn't know most of them, and the goggles weren't his—plus they were insanely expensive. "Sorry, guys," he told the other students as he reclaimed the goggles from Cassie and slipped them back on his head, the room seeming to light up for him like someone had cast a dim green spotlight across it. "We've got to find Kevin, and in order to do that I'll need to be able to see. Maybe later."

There was a lot of grumbling at that, but nobody could really argue—a lost classmate trumped playing with a nifty toy.

Malik patted Cassie on the shoulder, told her he'd see her later, and then rejoined Ilyana. The two of them headed back out into the hall.

"So where do you think Kevin might have gone?" Ilyana asked. "At least he's too tall to miss easily!" She laughed and answered the question Malik had been thinking but hadn't yet voiced. "He's in my social studies class."

"Nice. I've got no idea," Malik admitted. "But we know which way the front hall is, right?"

Ilyana pointed down the hall ahead of them. "Should be that way. We actually came around from the back."

"Okay, so we should just head toward the front, then," Malik suggested. "If Kevin was with them outside, but didn't make it all the way to this exhibit hall, he may've stopped off along the way."

"Makes sense," Ilyana agreed. "Let's follow the trail!"

There wasn't actually a trail, at least not one that Malik could see, but he followed her anyway as she headed off along the hall. There were doorways into other exhibit rooms every so often, sometimes on one side and sometimes on the other, and at each one they slowed to peer inside. One room had minerals and elements, the chips and slabs and hunks of stone and metal perched on long, thin metal rods so they could be studied from all sides. Another had all sorts of birds, both stuffed and skeletal. A third had pictures of stars and comets and asteroids.

A **comet** is an object in outer space that develops a long, bright "tail" when it passes near the Sun. Comets are made mostly of ice and dust. An **asteroid** is a rocky mass that orbits the Sun.

They were just passing an archway into a room so large their goggles couldn't penetrate the darkness when Malik paused. "Did you hear that?" he asked Ilyana.

She started to shake her head when they distinctly heard the sound of someone whimpering. "Oh, yeah," she whispered. They both crept toward the doorway as quietly as they could. Then Ilyana stopped. "What're we doing?" she asked, thwacking herself in the forehead with the palm of one hand. "This isn't a spy game! We're supposed to be helping him!"

"Yeah, you're right." Malik had gotten caught up in the weird notion of sneaking up on Kevin for some reason, but now he raised his voice instead. "Kevin?" he called out. "Yo, man, it's me, Malik. You in there?"

The whimpering had cut off, and after a few seconds a voice called out, "Malik? Where are you?"

"Just hang tight, bro," Malik replied. "We'll come to you, okay?"

He and Ilyana entered the room, no longer trying to sneak, and glanced around. Now that they were in the room, they could start to make out details, but at first those details didn't make any sense! There were what looked like glowing bars and beams everywhere! "What am I looking at?" Malik wondered aloud.

Beside him, Ilyana laughed. "Step back and glance up," she advised cryptically. Malik did—and gasped as a huge head suddenly loomed into view above him!

"What the—?" he started, but then realized what he was seeing. It was a dinosaur skull! They must have wandered into the dinosaur bones exhibit!

Now the bars and beams made sense. They were parts of various dinosaur skeletons, but he'd been seeing them too close-up to register the full shapes.

Malik stared up at the towering figures in awe. He'd seen dinosaur fossils before, of course, but even so they always amazed him. They had been so huge! Walking around beneath their fossils always made him feel like an ant or a fly, some tiny little creature just buzzing around and basically never drawing attention except as a possible pest. It was humbling.

But where was Kevin?

"Dude, where are you?" Malik called again.

"I have no idea," his friend replied shakily. "I can't see anything!" Dang, Malik thought. That made sense, but what were they going to do now? This room looked like it was huge!

But Ilyana had an idea. "Just keep talking," she advised. "We'll follow your voice!"

"Okay." Kevin said. Then he started humming. "How's that?"

"Perfect." Ilyana listened for a second and then tapped Malik on the shoulder and gestured to the left. He considered for a second, then nodded. Yes, it sounded like it was coming from that direction. They ventured that way together, moving slowly and carefully to avoid tripping over anything, and the humming definitely grew louder. They were going the right way!

After a few minutes, the humming sounded as if it were right in front of them. But where was Kevin? "Dude?" Malik asked the empty air.

"I'm here," came the reply. He was close! But Malik still couldn't see Kevin at all. All he saw were a bunch of bones, most of them upright like stair railings.

Then Ilyana gasped. "Look!" she said, and pointed.

Malik squinted in that direction and then stared.

There was a hand sticking out between the bones!

CHAPTER 9

A BONE TO PICK

"Kevin?"

Malik inched closer. Sure enough, now he could make out his friend's face behind the bones. But what was he doing in there? "You okay?"

"I think so," Kevin answered. "Where are you?"

"Right here." Malik reached out and grabbed Kevin's hand, making the other boy flinch before he returned the grip. "Gotcha!"

"Man, am I glad to see—well, hear—you!" Kevin responded. "But I think I'm trapped. I don't know how, though. It feels like I'm in a metal box or something, like there're bars all around me."

"Not bars," Ilyana corrected. She'd walked around the strange little prison. "Bones. You're pinned inside a dinosaur skeleton." Despite the strange situation, she grinned. "I think you somehow got yourself swallowed by a pteranodon."

A **pteranodon** is a kind of pterosaur, or flying dinosaur. The largest flying reptile of the late Cretaceous age, a pteranodon could have a wingspan as wide as eighteen feet but only weighed around seventy pounds. Pteranodons tended to eat mostly fish, though they would go after smaller dinosaurs if the opportunity presented itself.

Malik couldn't help but laugh. "How the heck did you do that, man?" he asked.

"I have no idea," his friend answered. "I didn't even know I was in the dinosaur room!" Malik could just see him shrug through the bones of his makeshift cage. "I was shutting off all the unnecessary lights," he explained. "Did you know they usually have all the lights on every day, just in case anyone wanders into that particular room? Do you know how much electricity they're wasting on lights that show off rooms nobody's going to see?"

"So you were falling behind everybody else because you were turning off all the lights," Ilyana summarized. "And then all the lights went out for real and you were stuck in the dark."

"Yeah," Kevin agreed. "I stumbled around a bit, bumped up against a few things, and then suddenly there was this loud noise all around me and bam! I was trapped!" He sighed. "I've been here ever since."

Malik frowned, studying the dinosaur skeleton trapping his friend. "It must have been hanging overhead," he reasoned, "and somehow it came down on top of you."

"The side wall's not far on that side," Ilyana pointed out, gesturing past them. "And there was something on the wall over there, like a big metal hook or something. Maybe that's what the ropes were tied to?"

"Could be," Malik agreed. "If they were, and Kevin bumped into them, he might've knocked them loose. Then that released the pteranodon, which came down—just as he stumbled through that spot on the floor." He winced. "You were lucky, man," he called out to Kevin. "It looks like you passed right through its rib cage. If you'd been a few feet to one side or the other, it would've slammed into you instead." And though the skeleton didn't look all that heavy, some of the bones ended in wicked tips.

"Great, lucky me," Kevin responded. "Now can you get me out of here?"

"Hold still," Ilyana warned.

"Oh, totally." Malik saw his friend frown. "Hey, who are you, anyway?"

"Oh, right," Ilyana replied. "It's me, Ilyana Desoff. We're in social studies together." The way she said it, so quietly, Malik thought she didn't expect Kevin to remember her.

But the taller boy was already nodding. "Oh, sure," he answered. "You're the one with all the movie references. Cool."

Ilyana beamed. "That's me!" She'd been studying the skeleton while they talked. "I don't know how we're going to get him out of that thing," she told Malik finally. "There doesn't look like there's enough room for him to crawl under it, or through it."

Malik had been thinking that as well. But he had another idea. "It fell down on top of him, right?" he asked. "So why don't we lift it back up?"

"Oh!" Ilyana clapped her hands together. "Great idea! The ropes would've been attached to a pulley. Even if they came loose from whatever they were tied to on the wall, if they're still on the pulley we should be able to haul it back up and get him out safely."

A **pulley** is a simple machine consisting of a wheel and a rope or cord that fits around it. You tie one end of the rope to something heavy and pull the other end—the wheel turns as you pull, allowing you to lift the heavy object more easily than if you were just picking it up by hand.

Together they walked around the dinosaur prison, searching the area. Malik moved in at one point and was able to see that yes, there was a rope attached near the top, between the shoulder blades. Now they just had to find the other end.

He actually walked right into the rope and brushed it from his face before he realized what it was. "Got it!" he shouted, grabbing at it and managing to latch on. The rope was dangling loose right at eye level, so all he'd seen was a blurry blob hovering in midair.

Ilyana quickly joined him, and together they reached up, grabbed ahold of the rope, and began to pull. "Stay perfectly still," Ilyana called to Kevin, "until we say otherwise."

"Got it," Kevin answered.

Between the two of them, Malik and Ilyana were able to pull the rope down a few feet. And, off to their side, the pteranodon rose accordingly.

"It's working!" Ilyana said excitedly. "Hold it there!" And, barely giving Malik time to tighten his grip, she ran over to check on Kevin. "Another few feet and he should be able to get out of the way."

"Great, let's do it." Malik was sweating a little— even though it wasn't super-heavy, hauling a dinosaur skeleton into the air wasn't easy! But he wrapped the rope around his hands for a better grip, and Ilyana grabbed on again, and together they yanked the rope down a few more feet. Then Malik planted his feet and held on while Ilyana went to check.

"Okay," he heard her tell Kevin, "I need you to duck down now. Here's my hand; grab it. Good, good. Okay, now walk toward me but don't straighten up. Perfect. Keep going, keep going—and you're out!"

Looking over his shoulder, Malik could just about make out two figures standing perhaps ten feet away. Whew! Now he just had to let the pteranodon

down easy—even though it was certainly preferable to letting Kevin get hurt, he figured the museum wouldn't be thrilled if he busted up their dinosaur. Plus, if it fell and shattered they could get hit by the pieces. Lowering it bit by bit, he was able to ease it back to the ground, and when it finally touched down he released the rope with a sigh. Wow, talk about a workout!

"Thanks, guys," Kevin told them as they led him from the room and back into the hall.

"No worries, dude," Malik told him. He reached out and grabbed Kevin's hand, then set that hand on his own shoulder. "Okay, we're gonna start back now, yeah? Just follow my lead. I'll shout if we're stopping or making a big turn, otherwise just keep your hand on my shoulder and we'll be fine."

Kevin nodded. "Got it."

The walk back felt like it took forever, since Malik had to go slowly so that Kevin could keep ahold of him. But finally they were back at the other room and guiding Kevin inside and over to an empty spot on the floor.

"Thank you so much for all your help," Mrs. Cavanaugh told them both. "And thank Mr. Enright for me as well."

"We will," Ilyana promised. Then the two of them headed back to their own exhibit hall quarters. They didn't talk much on the way. Malik wasn't sure why Ilyana had decided to keep quiet, but he was busy thinking about everything that'd gone on so far today. It'd been a crazy one, for sure! But cool, too. Even the blackout was giving them the chance to learn some nifty new things and play with some awesome technology. He laughed at himself, though he kept it quiet. No sense in admitting that he was almost glad the blackout had hit while they were here. How else would he have gotten to play with these goggles, or to go around to the other classes like that?

He wondered how long the blackout was going to last—and what else Mr. Enright had for them to learn if the darkness continued. Whatever it was, Malik was sure it was going to be pretty crazy.

CHAPTER 10

NOT THE WHOLE TRUTH

"Good morning, STEM class!"

Jules groaned and lifted her head out of her sleeping bag. It was past dawn, clearly, because even though the exhibit room lights were still out, everything was gray instead of pitch black, and she could clearly see the figure standing by the room's entrance, outlined by brighter light beyond. That same figure stepped into the room fully, and as Jules's eyes focused, she realized that it was Dr. Pillai. Their teacher had told them last night that the principal had stopped by while they were all out to let him know that the field trip would continue as planned despite the power outage.

"Off to a late start?" their principal asked Mr. Enright, who was already up and dressed even if his students weren't.

"Yes, well, given the excitement of last night I thought it best to let them sleep in," their teacher answered cheerfully. In truth, they'd all had a hard time falling asleep at all. For a few of them, like Tracey, it had simply been too dark. But something else had kept Jules awake, though she couldn't figure out what it was until Mr. Enright had offered a possible explanation:

"It's too quiet," he'd told them. They had all returned from checking in with the other classes and had taken turns using the nearby bathrooms to wash up for the night. Now they were all in their sleeping bags, which had been arrayed so that their feet all pointed inward and their heads radiated outward, as if they were the petals of an enormous flower.

"How can it be too quiet?" Chris had asked. "Isn't quiet a good thing when we're trying to sleep?"

"Well, too much noise would most likely keep you awake," their teacher had agreed from his own bedroll, "but a certain amount of sound can actually be soothing. You're all familiar with the concept of white noise, yes?" They'd all made noncommittal noises, including Jules—she knew she'd heard the term before, but she couldn't have said what it meant. "If we were being technical," Mr. Enright had continued, "white noise is a random signal with a constant power spectral density. What that means is that the sound is distributed over our entire hearing range. In other words, you cannot pick out any one sound or pattern

83

of sounds—instead, you hear a consistent low level of noise. It provides a pleasant background and helps to absorb other sounds that could actually keep you awake or wake you after you're asleep."

"So it's like a blanket of sound?" Malik had asked.

"Precisely!" Mr. Enright had exclaimed, and Jules could tell from his tone that their teacher was beaming. "And like a blanket, it's gentle and soothing and shields you from unwanted disturbance. Many people actually have white noise machines or white noise apps on their phones. But the rest of us still experience a certain degree of white noise because most electronics produce a low-level hum. When you're at home in your room, surrounded by your computer and your air conditioner and your phone charger, with your fridge downstairs and your furnace and hot water heater, your house is actually filled with white noise. And that helps you relax and fall asleep."

"But we don't have any of that now, because all the power's out," Jules had guessed aloud. "So we're not hearing anything, which actually means we're hearing every little noise separately."

"Quite so. That's why it's too quiet." Mr. Enright had rummaged around in his bag. "Fortunately, I have a solution to that." She'd heard him set something down on the hard marble floor, and an instant later a soft, steady hum had filled the room. "I brought a portable white noise generator," their teacher had explained. "And it's battery-powered."

Apparently that really had been the problem, because she'd fallen asleep shortly after that. And now she was having a hard time waking up completely.

"Yes, well, I simply wanted to check in on each class and see how everyone was doing," Dr. Pillai declared. She certainly didn't look like she'd had any trouble sleeping. Her suit was as smart and sharp as ever, and her hair was neatly braided—everything about her was perfectly placed. "I understand you went around to the other classes last night," she continued. "Thank you. The other teachers said they appreciated that, as did their students."

"Just doing our part to help," Mr. Enright assured her.

"Is the power still out?" Tracey asked, stretching and then covering her mouth as she let loose a powerful yawn.

Dr. Pillai frowned. "It is. I understand the power company is working on fixing that, but they think it could be another day or two before they can restore power." She shook her head. "At least this museum doesn't require climate control for any of its exhibits, so that's good."

"Climate control?" Malik asked. "What, you mean like an exhibit on ice?"

He was joking as usual, but their teacher took the question seriously. "That is in fact what she means, yes," he answered. "If there was an exhibit involving something frozen, for example, Ms. Dancy would have to worry about it melting now."

"Just like the food in a freezer," Chris said, and everyone nodded, remembering last night's discussion.

"Yes, well, hopefully we will have power again soon," Dr. Pillai continued. "In the meantime, you should conserve your remaining water as much as possible. It's probably best if you stayed in or near your assigned room as well—with the power out, alarms and security cameras aren't working, and although the police said they would send some off-duty officers over to keep an eye out just in case of potential looters, Ms. Dancy said it would be both safer and less worrisome if no one ventured out into the rest of the museum without the proper escort." She was eyeing Mr. Enright as she said this, as if expecting the tall science teacher to challenge her suggestions.

Instead, he offered her a graceful half-bow. "We will stay out of the other rooms," he agreed. "I would not want to worry Ms. Dancy."

Their principal continued to stare at him for a minute, frowning like she was trying to figure out what he was up to. But he just smiled back at her, and finally she nodded and turned away. They all listened to the clicking of her heels on the hard floors as she marched off out of sight.

As soon as she'd disappeared, Mr. Enright rubbed his hands together. "Right," he stated. "Time to get moving, class. Wash up, get dressed, and then pack everything back up and set it to the side. We have a great deal to do today and we are running behind, so we'll need to hustle."

Jules stared at him like he'd gone insane. "Get moving?" she asked. "Where're we going? You promised Dr. Pillai we wouldn't leave this room!"

"I did no such thing!" their teacher protested with a grin. "As you might recall, I told her none of you would venture into any other rooms here at the museum. Which you will not." His grin grew. "I said nothing about departing the museum altogether."

"We're leaving?" Ilyana asked. "But why?"

Mr. Enright laughed. "Not to worry," he said soothingly, "we should be back in plenty of time for the evening meal, not to mention lights out. As to where we're going, you'll just have to wait and see. All I'll tell you is that it relates directly to our conversation last night, and to current events here and in the region." He clapped his hands together. "Now let's go, please. Chop chop!"

Still grumbling a little, Jules crawled out of her sleeping bag. Then she dragged herself to her feet and started stretching to loosen up her sore muscles. Once she was feeling a bit more limber, Jules grabbed her backpack and pulled out the smaller bag containing today's clothes. Twenty minutes and a trip to the bathroom later, she felt a whole lot better, a bit cleaner, and definitely more awake.

"Everyone ready?" Mr. Enright asked. "Good. Follow me." He led them out of the room, down the corridor—away from the main hall—and finally to an unmarked steel fire exit. Jules tensed when her teacher reached for the bar but then relaxed and even mentally berated herself when the door opened without a sound. Of course, all of the alarms were off, as were the security cameras. It was the perfect time to sneak away.

They stepped outside—just as a familiar-looking school bus pulled up nearby. Its front door opened, and a cheerful, hairy face peered out at them from the driver's seat.

"Bud!" Jules shouted happily, as did the rest of her class. Randall harrumphed but turned away quickly to hide what Jules was pretty sure was a big smile at the sight of their chimpanzee mascot.

"What're you doing here, man?" Malik asked as he climbed onboard the bus. He and Bud exchanged high-fives.

"I contacted him this morning and told him we would be needing the bus," Mr. Enright answered for the chimp, "and told him where and when to meet us."

"Oh, that reminds me," Tracey said, pulling out her cell phone. "I'd better call home—my mom gets worried if I don't check in once in a while." All the other kids copied her, but Jules knew her frown mirrored their own when a minute later she discovered that her phone wasn't working.

"Zero bars?" Malik complained, holding his phone up and turning in a slow circle. "How is that even possible? This is the United States—aren't we guaranteed good phone service or something?"

The others all laughed at him. "There's no power, remember?" Jules reminded him. "That means no cell towers, which means no phone service."

A **cell tower** is a radio mast, tower, or other tall structure with antennae and electrical communications equipment. This equipment provides radio and phone service to an area of land, called a cell.

"Actually, all cell towers are encouraged to have a battery or backup generator in case the electrical grid loses power," Mr. Enright corrected Jules. "The government tried requiring at least eight hours, but they couldn't get the bill passed, so there isn't anything saying towers *have* to have backups. Most of them do anyway, but they tend to have only enough for about four hours. And since the power went out last night—"

"They've used that up already," Jules finished. "Swell."

"Here." Mr. Enright pulled out an old-fashioned flip phone and handed it to Tracey. "You can take turns using it to call home."

"Hey, how come you still have service?" Malik asked when he saw Tracey dial the phone, smile, and start talking to someone on the other end. Jules noticed that the phone had a thick built-in antenna along one side.

"It's a sat phone," their teacher explained. "That's short for satellite phone. It connects directly to orbiting satellites instead of using local cellular towers, so as long as the phone has a charge and there's at least one functional satellite somewhere overhead, it has a signal."

"Smart," Malik admitted. The others agreed.

"It pays to be prepared," Mr. Enright replied. "For example, this bus is a hybrid. That means it gets better gas mileage than a regular bus and doesn't need to refuel as often. Do you know why that's important during a blackout?"

A **hybrid car** has both a gasoline engine with a fuel tank and an electric motor with one or more batteries and this vehicle can use either for propulsion. The word "hybrid" means a mix of two different things.

It was Chris who raised his hand. "Because the pumps are all electric," he answered. "So if there's no power, you can't get gas even though the gas itself is fine. Just like with water and the water treatment plants."

Mr. Enright nodded. "Exactly." The last student finished calling home and returned the sat phone to him. Mr. Enright pocketed it again and then gestured toward the bus seats. "Now buckle up. We need to be extra careful right now. After all, the traffic lights aren't working either!"

Jules wondered where their teacher was taking them when nothing was working. Wherever it was, she hoped it was worth the trip!

CHAPTER 11

BUS-TED!

"Why can't they design gas pumps that don't need electricity?" Ilyana asked as Bud put the bus in gear and they pulled away from the museum. Malik still had to remind himself that the chimpanzee wasn't actually driving—the bus had an advanced robotic system and drove itself provided you programmed the destination into it ahead of time. But Bud liked to sit in the driver's seat and work the door controls and grip the wheel.

"Gas pumps didn't originally need electricity," Mr. Enright answered, twisting around in his seat to face the rest of them. "Back when the first gas pumps appeared in the 1920s, they were actual pumps—the gas was in a storage tank below the pump, and you used a long handle to pump it up into the hose and from there to your car. They developed electric pumps in the 1930s, adding fans to push the gas up out of the tank and through the pump to the hose. Now, of course, it's all computerized, which makes it far easier to operate—unless the power goes out, at which point you're stuck wishing for one of those old manual pumps again."

Ilyana's question was a good one, but Malik had one that was even better. "Why do we need gasoline at all?" he asked their teacher. "If water plants need electricity to run, don't you need power for whatever they use to create gasoline? So even if you could get a pump that worked without power, during a long-term blackout you wouldn't have any gas to fill the pump. We'd be better off finding some other way to run the bus—and everyone else's cars and trucks and all that."

"Those are excellent questions," Mr. Enright complimented him. "And to answer them, yes, there are vehicles that require even less gas than this bus. For example, you could have an electric car. Those have batteries that you plug in to charge, just like your laptop or phone. You can plug them into special charging stations, but usually you can plug them into a regular wall outlet as well; it will simply take longer for them to recharge from there. Theoretically, you could plug an electric car into a portable generator, which means you would still be able to charge your car during a blackout."

"What do those generators run on, though?" Chris asked. "Aren't they gas powered?"

"Many of them, yes," their teacher admitted. "Some are not, however. I'll explain more about that when we reach our destination." He had a little smile on his face, like he was extremely pleased with himself, and Malik could tell that asking more questions wouldn't do him any good. Mr. Enright had a surprise planned, and he wasn't about to let any of them ruin it.

Just then the shrill wail of a siren cut through the morning air. Glancing out the window, Malik saw a police car right behind them, its lights flashing. But why? he wondered. Could the cops have seen Bud sitting in the driver's seat and thought he was really driving the bus? Or was this about something else?

"Sir, the authorities are onto us," Randall announced from his seat at the back. "If this mission is need-to-know only, I suggest evasive maneuvers."

"I don't think that'll be necessary, Randall, but thank you," their teacher replied. "I'll handle this."

Handle it? Malik thought, exchanging a glance with Chris. These were the cops. How was their science teacher going to "handle" them?

"Better pull over, Bud," he heard Mr. Enright quietly tell their chimpanzee chauffeur. "Then hop in the back and let me do the talking." That made sense, Malik thought. He couldn't imagine that, assuming that wasn't the reason for stopping the bus in the first place, the cops would be too happy about finding a chimpanzee at the wheel!

Bud nodded vigorously, showing his teeth. He pushed a button and twisted the wheel as the bus began to slow and pull to the side. Despite watching closely, Malik still couldn't be completely sure the chimp hadn't done all that manually—was there really a "slow down and pull over" button on the dash? As soon as the bus had come to a stop, Bud hopped out of the chair over the back, then jumped from seat to seat until he was all the way in the back row. At the same time, as soon as he'd cleared that first spot, Mr. Enright slid forward and dropped into the driver's seat. By the time the police officers had reached them and tapped on the window, their teacher looked like he'd been driving the bus all morning, so much so that Malik actually shook his own head, not sure if what he felt outweighed what he'd seen.

Someone tapped on the bus's front door, and Mr. Enright hit the lever. A second later a young police officer stepped onto the bus.

"License and registration, please," he asked, and Mr. Enright complied without a word, just passing the two items to the cop straightaway. Now Malik could see someone else outside by the bus's open door, and he guessed that this would be the first cop's partner, who was hanging back in case there was trouble. The first officer examined Mr. Enright's papers for a minute and then handed them back.

"Where are you going with these kids?" The cop asked next. His eyes were touching on everything, particularly Malik and the others. What was the cop looking for, though?

"This is my science class," Mr. Enright explained. "Our entire grade at Einstein High is having a sleepover at the natural history museum this weekend. But the power went out there, and so we were one of several classes tasked with traveling to the store and purchasing food and a handful of other must-have items the students might need."

"Einstein High?" The cop repeated. "Who's your principal?"

Mr. Enright sighed. "Dr. Pillai." He leaned in a little and lowered his voice as if he was sharing a secret. "She's maybe not the friendliest boss, but she's good at her job."

"And she sent you out here?" The cop had his phone out like he was going to dial someone.

"She did," their teacher answered. "You can call her and confirm that. I've got her number here." He reached into his back pocket—slowly—and pulled out his wallet, extracting a business card, which he handed over to the officer.

The officer took the card and studied it for a minute, even going so far as to punch the number into his phone. But he didn't raise the phone to his ear, which made Malik think he hadn't actually hit the call button.

"It's not safe to be out on the road during a blackout," the cop declared after a second. "No traffic lights, so people tend to either sit at the light waiting for it to change—even though it never will—or go whenever they want and no matter what other cars are doing around them. Get near either one of those and you've got a really good chance of getting into an accident." He glanced around at the bus. "And this thing isn't going to turn on a dime, or stop on one."

"I understand completely," Mr. Enright assured the policeman. "And we would never have risked braving traffic unassisted if not for the desperate need to feed over a hundred students." He hit the cop with his best grin before continuing, "I don't suppose you have any recommendations to add to the grocery list?"

For a second, the officer just stared at him. Then he, too, broke into a smile. "Hot dogs," he answered finally, pocketing his phone again. "Quick, easy, you can cook a whole bunch up at once, never met a kid who didn't like 'em."

"That's precisely what we were thinking," Mr. Enright replied. "But always good to have another vote in favor."

The cop handed him back his license and the bus registration, along with the business card. "Just be careful, okay?" he urged as he turned to go. "We tell people to stay inside unless they really need to be out, and to walk unless they have to drive, but that doesn't stop many from driving anyway, and the more people there are on the road when we don't have lights in place, the more dangerous it gets for everyone."

"We definitely will," their teacher promised. "Thank you, officer."

The policeman waved as he exited the bus, and he and his partner stood there watching as Mr. Enright put the bus in gear and slowly pulled away.

"Whoa," Chris said after they'd been driving for a few minutes. "That was crazy."

"Yeah, and you lied to that cop," Tracey added. "You said we were out here getting food, but we aren't, are we?"

"We might," their teacher answered easily as he slowed to a stop at an intersection. There weren't any other cars in sight, but he waited a full ten seconds anyway before putting the bus into motion again. "But no, that isn't where we're going at the moment."

"Shouldn't we have stayed inside, like he said?" Malik asked. "I mean, he's right—the idea of people driving around with no traffic signals is pretty scary."

"I've driven in far worse places," Mr. Enright assured them. "Believe me, this is nothing compared to maneuvering a tank through the bazaar in Morocco in the middle of the afternoon. Besides, if you want to learn about power and electricity during a blackout, you can't simply pull up a website on your computer, can you? You have to go to the places in question in person, and that's precisely what we're doing."

"Assuming we make it there in one piece," Malik muttered, sitting back in his seat. But if his teacher heard, he didn't reply. Bud chittered at him, however, as he climbed over one of the other benches to drop down onto the seat next to Malik. The chimp put an arm around his shoulder and grinned at him, as if to say "don't worry, I'll make sure you're safe."

"Yeah, thanks, Bud," Malik told the chimp. "You're a pal."

The chimp nodded vigorously in reply. That didn't make Malik feel any better, however, or any more comfortable about their little outing. He knew that Mr. Enright took a relaxed view toward danger—he'd proved that when he'd taken them out to a floodplain last month and set them to work clearing flooded houses! But deliberately driving around during a blackout just seemed like a really bad idea, and Malik didn't even know why they were doing it.

He assumed Mr. Enright would tell them where they were going and why eventually. Provided they made it there—wherever *there* was!

CHAPTER 12

A LIGHT IN THE DARK

A few minutes later, Tracey pointed out the window. "Hey, check it out!" she announced. "That building up ahead has its lights on!"

Jules followed her friend's gesture, and, sure enough, they were approaching a large, low building set well back from the road—and even from here she could see the lights gleaming out of its windows. But a quick glance around confirmed that the street lights were still out, and that all the other buildings around them were dark. So how did this one still have power?

"That's where we're going, isn't it?" she guessed aloud. "The one that still has power?"

"It is indeed," Mr. Enright confirmed. He was still driving and seemed to be enjoying the task—Jules was sure she'd heard him humming under his breath a few times. "And a good thing too—they wouldn't be very good at their jobs if they couldn't even manage to keep their own lights on at a time like this!"

He pulled the bus into a large circular driveway in front of the building, then parked there right by the front doors. "All right, everybody out," he announced, working the door lever. "You see, all in one piece," he continued to nobody in particular, but Jules thought she saw Malik redden a bit. What was that about?

Randall was on his feet as soon as the bus turned off, of course, and started bellowing, "Right, everybody off the bus on the double! Let's go, troops, time's a-wasting!" in typical Randall fashion. With a sigh, Jules slid out of her seat and joined the others in exiting. For once, Bud didn't stay with the bus but walked off with Malik, holding his hand like a trusting child. Mr. Enright came last and pushed a button to close the bus doors behind him.

A man was standing by the front doors waiting for them. He was tall, as tall as Mr. Enright but considerably wider, and his white lab coat was stretched so tight over the shoulders that it would've made a football player proud. He had wildly curly black hair, which seemed to reach in every direction like a plant seeking sunlight, and a bushy black mustache.

"Good morning!" he called out in a loud, cheerful voice as soon as they were all standing on solid ground. "And welcome! I'm Doctor Don Deere, and this"—he swept an arm behind him to indicate the building—"is the Alternative Energy Research Institute. Or, as we like to call it, the AERIE."

"Airy?" Malik asked. "You mean, like 'breezy,' as in 'it sure is airy out here'?"

Dr. Deere chuckled. "Nice one! No, it's pronounced 'airy' but it's actually spelled A-E-R-I-E. That's what you call a nest for eagles, falcons, hawks, or other birds of prey. Typically, it's a high-up spot somewhere in the mountains or in a tall tree, but we're a little more grounded here." He chuckled at his own word play, and so did Jules. Dr. Deere reminded her of her dad, big and beefy enough to be intimidating but too nice of a guy to be scary.

Dr. Deere and Mr. Enright were shaking hands, and it was clear that they already knew each other. It had been the same way with the scientists who'd been called in to deal with the flash flood, Jules remembered. Was there anyone their teacher didn't know?

"Good to see you again, Todd," Dr. Deere said, clapping their teacher on the shoulder with one huge hand. "It's been, what, since that thing on the International Space Station?"

"Indeed," Mr. Enright agreed. "That was a bit of a scare, eh? Especially when those rockets wouldn't fire!"

"Yeah, and squeezing into that Chinese capsule wasn't any fun, either!" the big scientist remembered, shaking his head. "I kept thinking they were gonna

have to chop me off at the knees to fit me in there!"
Both men laughed while Jules and the others waited
patiently for them to finish reminiscing.

"I called Dr. Deere this morning to let him know
we'd be stopping by," Mr. Enright explained after
they'd calmed back down and he'd turned to face the
class. "You wanted to know what else we could use
for power besides gas? Well, this is the place to get
that answered."

"Absolutely," Dr. Deere agreed. "Come on, I'll
give you guys the grand tour." And he led them inside.
He did raise an eyebrow when he saw Bud, but he
didn't say anything, or try to stop the chimp from
joining them, which made Jules like the big scientist
even more.

The AERIE was only one story tall, it seemed, but
it was basically a single huge room with a really high
ceiling, so stepping inside the building did in fact feel
very "airy." Most of the ceiling's central portion was
glass, Jules noticed, which let in a lot of sunlight, but
there were actual lights along the walls as well, and big
fluorescent light fixtures hung in rows from the ceiling
on either side. The floor was rubber and felt oddly
springy as she walked.

Several other people were working on projects
around the room—in a lot of ways it reminded Jules of
their STEM classroom, with its small lab tables spaced

out so that people could gather at each one, either to listen to Mr. Enright lecture from the front of the room or to work on projects individually or in small groups. This room was large enough that you could easily have a dozen projects going on at once and still have plenty of space between them. And because the ceiling was so high, sound seemed to get swallowed up—she could see people talking in several spots but couldn't make out more than a faint murmur of conversation.

"Just like our name suggests, we research alternative forms of energy," Dr. Deere explained. "Specifically, we focus on renewable resources. Do you guys know what a nonrenewable resource is?"

Ilyana's hand shot up. "That's where it only exists in a finite quantity, right?" she asked. "So it gets used up and then it's gone."

The big scientist beamed at her. "That's right! Unfortunately, most of our power today is based on nonrenewable resources. Like gas, oil, and coal. Anybody know what gasoline comes from?"

This time it was Tracey who answered. "It's petroleum-based," their resident gearhead answered. Of course she would know that, Jules thought.

"Absolutely," Dr. Deere agreed. "And petroleum is a compound made up of various hydrocarbons, mostly alkanes like paraffin and cycloalkanes like naphthalene. It's a fossil fuel, which means it's basically the liquefied remains of ancient organic materials, mostly algae and zooplankton. Petroleum is created by intense heat and pressure compressing and melting those materials for centuries. Which is why it's nonrenewable—it takes a ridiculously long time to create petroleum, longer than the entire human race has been around, so it's not like we can just produce more. There's a certain amount in the world, and once that's gone, it's gone."

"Isn't oil also from fossils?" Jules asked.

Dr. Deere nodded. "Oil, at least the kind of oil that's used for heating and for running things like cars and generators, is also a petrochemical—it comes from petroleum, just like gasoline. Actually, oil refineries take the petroleum, which is also known as crude oil, and separate that out into things like gasoline, butane, kerosene, and other derivatives." He raised an eyebrow. "Here's a fun fact: did you know that a single forty-two-gallon barrel of crude oil can be split into about nineteen gallons of gasoline, ten gallons of diesel fuel, four gallons of jet fuel, three gallons of heavy fuel oil and liquefied petroleum gas, two gallons of heating oil, and seven gallons of other products?"

Chris proved yet again that he was the fastest of them when it came to math. "That's forty-five gallons!" he exclaimed. "Out of forty-two! How does that even make any sense?"

"Especially when some of what's drained off the crude oil should be useless sludge?" the scientist agreed. "It's because they cut the derivatives with other additives, so a lot of that has various extra chemicals in it, either to help it work better or just to act as filler."

A **derivative** is something that is based on or comes from another substance.
An **additive** is a substance that you add to another, usually to improve it in some way. Foods often contain additives to enhance flavor or to act as preservatives.

"And coal?" Ilyana asked. "You said that was a nonrenewable resource too?"

"It sure is," Dr. Deere replied. "Coal is basically just fossilized carbon, though of course the process to form it is a lot more complicated than that. Basically dead plant matter gets turned into peat, which turns into lignite, which becomes subbituminous coal, then bituminous coal, then anthracite. It's the anthracite that we actually mine and use. People have been mining coal and burning it for fuel as far back as 1000 BCE, and it's still the single biggest source of energy for electricity in the world. Most of our coal comes from China these days, with the U.S. coming in second as a coal producer. The only problem is, we burn through the stuff—literally!—at a crazy rate. And just like petroleum, it takes thousands of years to make more."

"That's why you're looking for alternatives," Malik ventured. "Especially ones that are renewable instead."

The scientist nodded. "Exactly right. Do you know why bamboo has become so popular in wooden floors over the last few years?" All of them shook their heads. "Because it takes twenty to fifty years for an oak or a maple, or even a pine, to reach maturity so it can be harvested for wood. Bamboo can be harvested after only six to ten years. And because harvesting bamboo doesn't kill the plant the way harvesting a tree does, you can harvest bamboo every year if you're careful. That's why it's a renewable resource. If you take proper precautions you could manage to never significantly reduce the total amount in the world." He winked. "That's what we're looking to do with energy—find sources that we can use without destroying or reducing them."

"Have you found any yet?" Jules asked, then clapped a hand over her mouth, shocked at her own audacity. These were grown men and women, talented scientists, and she was just a high school girl. What right did she have to ask such a bold question?

But Dr. Deere didn't seem to mind. Instead, he beamed at her. "Have we ever!" he replied, laughing. "Would you like to see what we've come up with so far?"

Jules nodded eagerly. All around her, she saw the rest of her class doing the same. Real sources of renewable energy—that was definitely worth the drive out here, even in a blackout!

CHAPTER 13

SUNNY DAYS

D r. Deere led them over to one end of the room, where a group of other scientists were working around several long tables. "This is Doctor Wilma Buchannan," he told them, tapping a woman on the shoulder. "She's our head of photovoltaic research."

Dr. Buchannan turned toward them. She was small, maybe Malik's height, and African American, with dark skin, close-cropped dark hair, and a pretty heart-shaped face. "Hi there," she greeted them all warmly. "Always nice to meet young people interested in science, and especially in alternate energy."

"What's photovoltaic mean?" Ilyana asked. "I'm sure I've read that term before."

"Probably," Dr. Buchannan agreed, "considering it's been around since the 1850s."

Malik gasped, as did the others. 1850! That was over a hundred and sixty years ago!

The petite scientist was still speaking. "It comes from the Greek word for light and from the term 'volt,' which is a unit of electromotive force and is named after Alessandro Volta, who invented the first battery. It means the process of converting sunlight to usable electricity."

"You're talking about solar power, right?" Malik asked. "My dad has a solar-powered calculator, and I know a guy who's got a solar charger for his phone. But you're saying solar power's been around since 1850?"

Dr. Buchannan smiled at him. "That sounds ridiculous, doesn't it? You're wondering why, if we've had solar cells for so long, we don't use them for everything?" She shook her head. "The truth is, scientists *have* been developing them for almost that long. A scientist named Alexandre Edmond Becquerel first coined the phrase 'photovoltaic effect' in 1839. The first paper on solar cells was published by W.G. Adams and R.E. Day in 1877. Augustin Mouchot showed off a solar power generator in Paris in 1873." She frowned. "The problem was, it was really expensive to produce such devices, at least back then. And they weren't very efficient. Charles Fritts developed what was really the first true solar cell in 1883, but it had less than 1 percent efficiency—that means it could convert less than 1 percent of the sunlight it absorbed into electricity. That's not very useful—we'd need a solar cell the size of this building just to recharge your phone!"

Jules nodded. "So you've been working on ways to improve that efficiency?" she guessed.

"Not just me!" Dr. Buchannan laughed. "Lots of people have worked on solar power over the years. And we've come a long way already. When NASA sent up the Vanguard satellite in 1958, they included solar panels to help power it. Solar cells are still the main power source for most of our orbital satellites and a lot of our space probes, because out in space there aren't any size restrictions so you can have giant solar panels, which don't weigh much and can absorb sunlight without any interference from Earth's atmosphere. And the more advances are made in semiconductors, circuit boards, batteries, and other related areas, the cheaper it gets to produce solar cells. That's been a big help, but we're constantly looking for new ways to lower costs and improve efficiency so we can provide more power with less space and for less money."

"So how does it work?" Chris asked.

"I'll show you." The scientist stepped aside so they could see the various tools and objects set out on the table next to her. "Solar cells are very simple, really. Sunlight is absorbed through a semiconductor, most commonly silicon. That absorbed energy knocks loose electrons within the semiconductor. An electric field forces the loose electrons to flow in a particular direction. This produces a current. Then all you have to do is attach metal contacts to the top and bottom of the solar cell and draw off that current. That's how a battery works, supplying current to power devices like a phone."

A **semiconductor** is a solid substance that is not normally a good conductor of electricity, or a good insulator against it, but becomes a much better conductor when heat, light, or voltage is applied.
An **electron** is a stable subatomic particle with a negative electrical charge.

"That does sound simple," Malik agreed. He laughed. "I'm betting there's a lot more to it than that, though."

"Absolutely," Dr. Buchannan agreed. "For example, as I said, we tend to use silicon for our semiconductors. That's because silicon has an unusual crystalline structure. Each silicon atom has fourteen electrons, arranged into three shells. The first shell holds only two electrons. The second shell holds eight. The third holds four—but has room for four more. So what happens in silicon crystals is the atoms share electrons with their neighbors, basically borrowing an electron from its four closest friends to make up the rest of its outermost shell. That's important because we mix other elements in with the silicon and they share electrons, but if we do it right, there are a few loose electrons left over."

"Huh?" Malik rubbed at his face. Given the looks on his friends' faces, he wasn't the only one getting a little confused here.

Dr. Buchannan laughed. "Look at it this way," she explained. "Let's say we add some phosphorous to our silicon. Phosphorous has five electrons in its outer shell. The silicon only wants to borrow four. That leaves one electron without a buddy, just wandering around aimlessly. Got it?" Malik and the others nodded. "So in our silicon-phosphorous mix, we have one free electron. That's where we get our negative electrons from. On the other side, we mix silicon with boron, which has only three electrons in its outer shell, so we wind up with positive electrons wandering free over there. Put them together and the negative electrons try to fill the holes on the positive side, which creates an electrical field. Light contains photons, and those break apart the energy pairs in our silicon, increasing the electric field as it forces all the negative electrons to the positive side. That's the current. But we're only getting one electron from each mixture, which isn't a lot. That's why the cells aren't all that efficient."

A **photon** is the fundamental particle of visible light—basically a packet of electromagnetic energy.

"How efficient are they?" Tracey wanted to know.

The scientist nodded to show that was a good question. "Most solar cells these days have only about 20 percent efficiency," she answered. "We've been able to get some as high as 40 percent. The problem is that we can only use part of the sunlight to power our cells. Visible light is actually made up of different colors— you know that, right?"

"Sure," Ilyana responded. "Roy G. Biv. Red, orange, yellow, green, blue, indigo, and violet." Malik raised an eyebrow at her, and she shrugged. "There was a comic book villain named the Rainbow Raider, and his name was Roy G. Bivalow," she said with a grin. "It stuck."

Malik laughed and shook his head. "Hey, I guess comic books *are* educational!"

Dr. Buchannan was laughing as well but nodding too. "I learned a lot from comic books, back when I was a kid," she confided. "Great vocabulary, and some of those early superheroes were scientists themselves! Anyway, the different colors have different wavelengths. Some of those pass right through the solar cells. Some of them don't have enough energy to affect them. Some have too much energy. Only a few wavelengths are just right. We call that the band gap energy of a material. The lower the band gap, the more photons will affect our cells but the lower the voltage, so we need to balance that out, finding the lowest gap that still produces enough voltage to provide a decent amount of power. Right now we're losing about 70 percent of the power actually available in sunlight. Then there's resistance from the silicon itself, because it's only a semiconductor rather than a true conductor—it loses energy as the electrons flow from one side of the cell to the other. We use a metallic contact grid to shorten the distance the electrons have to travel, leaving the rest of the cell open so photons can enter in the first place, but we still block some and leak others."

"It's all a big balancing act, then?" Tracey asked. "You have to find ways to get the most efficiency from each part of the process?"

"That's it in a nutshell." Dr. Buchannan waved her hand at the table and its contents. "We're trying different mixtures of silicon and other elements, different conductors, different backings, different connectors, everything we can think of. There are lots of interesting new ideas out there right now. For example, a lot of solar cells rely upon elements like tellurium, gallium, and indium. Those are all rare earths, though, so they're expensive and hard to come by. People are trying cells with other elements now, like copper and zinc, ones that are a lot cheaper and a lot easier to find."

She indicated one corner of the table, where a pair of scientists were bent over a grid of what looked like watch batteries—small metal discs laid out on a square. Except they were actually looking at a screen, Malik realized, and the object itself, which sat on a glass plate below the screen, was maybe the size of his thumb!

"That's a quantum dot solar cell," Dr. Buchannan explained. "It's using quantum dots instead of the traditional silicon cells. These dots act like artificial atoms, but we can tune their energy levels by changing their size. That means we can also adjust their band gap. We can grow quantum cells at different sizes, depending upon which band gap we want, from far infrared on down. Half the solar energy that reaches Earth is in the infrared, so by using these we've got access to part of the spectrum we could never use before. And we can use quantum dots to produce what we call multijunction solar cells, which can absorb several different wavelengths at once. Normal single-junction cells can get up to about 34 percent efficiency. A multijunction cell could get as high as 85 percent, we think."

"That's huge, right?" Malik asked. "Eighty-five percent?"

"It *is* huge," the scientist agreed. "We're not there yet, but we're working on it." She sighed. "Current estimates say that we have over sixty-nine billion square feet of residential rooftops available in the U.S. alone. If we could use all of that for solar panels, we could generate at least half the electricity this country needs, maybe more. And with cells made from zinc and copper, those panels could be cheap enough that everyone could afford to buy them and install them." Then she grinned at them. "In fact, one of our goals is to make solar panels so cheap and so useful that people can't afford *not* to use them! It'll be like the idea of having running water in your house—there are so many good things about it, and so few bad, that it'd be silly to ever consider not having it there."

Jules had a question. "Is that what's keeping the lights on in here?" she asked, gesturing up at the ceiling and the skylights there. "Solar panels on the roof?"

"That's part of it," Dr. Buchannan answered. "It's not the only thing we've got going on here, though." She laughed. "My photovoltaic group is just one part of our work at AERIE. Some of the others are looking into other options that are just as exciting."

"Ha, I never thought I'd hear you admit that!" Dr. Deere called out. He'd been standing off to one side, listening. Now he clapped a hand on Dr. Buchannan's shoulder—he was over a foot taller than her, and his hand looked huge there, but she didn't seem to mind. "The work Dr. Buchannan is doing is amazing," he told them, "and sunlight is easily the most available energy source we have. Over the whole planet we're getting somewhere around eighty-four terawatts from the sun each day. The world only uses about twelve terawatts a day for all its power needs. That's the entire world. So if we could convert and use even one-fifth of that solar energy, we could power the entire planet on solar power alone!"

"That sure beats my dad's phone charger!" Malik joked. Everyone laughed, including the two scientists.

"It does, but that charger is a start," Dr. Deere pointed out. "Come on, I'll introduce you to a few of the others and they can tell you what resources they're working on."

As he led them toward a different corner of the room, Malik couldn't help glancing back at Dr. Buchannan and her team. When his dad had first brought home his solar phone charger, Malik had thought that was pretty sweet—a little hand-sized platter you set out on the windowsill, which could charge your phone from sunlight alone. But the idea of those panels all over the house, powering everything in it, was mind-blowing. And on a day like today—with the sun shining overhead but most of the city's buildings and homes dark and powerless—well, he could easily see why they were so excited about the possibilities!

CHAPTER 14

CATCHING THE LIGHT

Just then, Jules heard a strange noise overhead. She glanced up, frowning as she squinted against the sunlight streaming in through the glass. What had she heard? It had sounded like a creaking, but with the shrill bite of metal against metal.

After a second, she noticed that one of the fluorescent fixtures was swaying slightly. What was that all about? This was California, so they were used to earthquakes, but she hadn't felt any tremors.

Then she spotted a small, dark shape atop the fixture, like an extra shadow.

A shadow wearing a bright orange flight suit.

Sure enough, when she did a quick survey of their group, someone small and hairy was noticeably absent.

Others had started hearing the noise as well and were also peering up at the ceiling.

"It's Bud," Jules called out. "He's up on that light fixture!"

Now they were all staring. "Bud!" Malik shouted up to the chimp. "Get down from there!"

"I'm sorry about this," Mr. Enright told Dr. Deere. "He's usually so well behaved, but I think the blackout's been putting him on edge like everyone else. And when he gets anxious he reverts to old habits. Like swinging from trees."

The AERIE head waved off the apology. "I'm more worried about him than about anything he might do," he answered, eyes fixed on the chimp high above. "Those fixtures aren't rated to hold any extra weight."

Malik was still yelling up to Bud, as were a few of the others, and it was clear the chimp had heard them, because he stopped swinging and leaned out from the light fixture to chitter something back down to them. He had one hand and one foot wrapped securely around the chain holding that end of the fixture up, but when he moved Jules heard the screech of metal again.

"I don't think that's going to hold!" Ilyana cried out. "He's got to get down from there!"

"Bud, you need to move!" Malik instructed. "Now!" He waved his arm toward the next fixture in line.

Bud nodded and released the chain. Then he scampered across the fixture—which groaned alarmingly at even his slight weight—and, when he reached its far end, swung out from the chain there.

122

With his other hand he grabbed ahold of the next fixture's chain and pulled himself across. It was like watching a circus high-wire act!

Chris was watching the chimp's forward motion. "He should be fine as long as he keeps moving," he offered, not taking his eyes off Bud for a second. "He's redistributing his weight, so it's never settling in one spot long enough to cause a problem."

But even though Bud was now off that first fixture, it continued to screech and shake. "He's weakened the supports," Dr. Deere explained, his voice still calm even though his eyes were a little wild with alarm. "Even though he's not putting any additional weight on it now, that fixture is definitely going to fall. It's only a matter of time."

Jules studied the fixture and shuddered at the thought of it plummeting toward them. It was just a basic metal frame, with big hooks up top for the support chains and three long fluorescent tubes down the underside. Those tubes had to be at least six feet long, though, and when they fell they would send glass flying everywhere!

"We have to stop it from breaking," she said more to herself than to anyone else. But Mr. Enright heard her.

"An excellent idea," he agreed, waving the rest of the class closer. "What would you suggest we do?"

Jules looked to her classmates. "We've got to find a

way to keep those lights from hitting the ground," she explained.

"Or the tables beneath it," Ilyana added. "That would shatter them just as easily."

"We could try lassoing them," Malik suggested, staring up at the light. "If we could hook the end where the chain's pulling loose, maybe we could use a pulley system to keep it up there?" But even as he said it, he shook his head. "Nah, no way to do that outside a Western flick," he admitted.

"We could get really strong fans and direct them up at the ceiling right below the light," Chris offered. "That could keep them from falling, or at least slow them down so we could somehow get them to the ground intact. People practice skydiving over fans like that—if one's strong enough to keep a two-hundred-pound person floating, it should be able to handle that fixture."

Dr. Deere had been following the conversation. "That would work," he agreed, "if we had any fans like that. But we don't, I'm afraid."

What do we have, Jules wondered, looking around, even as Tracey asked, "Well how would you normally keep something that's falling from hitting the ground and breaking?"

"Grab it before it hits," Malik repeated, though his expression said he knew that wasn't really an option here.

"Create enough lift to keep it off the ground," Chris added, just to keep the list going.

Tracey was frowning, however. "If we were firefighters," she suggested slowly, "we'd use a trampoline to catch people who had to jump from a burning building. Or some kind of inflatable cushion to break their fall so they could reach the ground safely."

"Very good," Mr. Enright told her. "That's right. Firefighters use those tools to help people reduce their own momentum, redirecting the force of their fall so when they do hit the ground, it's gentle enough that they don't get hurt."

Momentum is the force that keeps an object in motion after it has started moving.

"We need a trampoline, then," Jules said. She shook her head. "I'm not seeing anything like that around here." But then she spotted a table off to one side that had been covered over, either to protect its contents from being seen or just to keep them from getting dusty. "What about that?" she asked, indicating the heavy cloth cover.

The others all followed her gesture. "Perfect!" Malik announced. "We can hold it taut between us, right under the fixture, and when it falls the cloth will absorb the impact!"

Mr. Enright nodded. "I believe we have a plan," he declared. He tapped Jules and Tracey on the shoulders. "Quickly, grab the cloth! The rest of you, come with me!"

Jules hurried over to get the cloth, her friend right beside her. They were careful to lift it straight up as much as possible, so as not to disturb or damage the delicate equipment it had been covering. When they turned to find the others, they saw why Mr. Enright had split the class up. Everyone else was busy lifting and moving one of the heavy work tables off to one side. It was the one that was directly beneath the damaged fixture.

"We'd have had a hard time holding the tarp over the table," Mr. Enright explained as Jules and Tracey rejoined the others and everyone grabbed an edge of the cloth. "This way we have more room beneath it, which means it can absorb more momentum."

They spaced themselves out where the table had been and stared up at the fixture. Its creaking and screeching sounds had grown louder and more frequent as they'd worked, and now the noise was a near constant. Jules flinched as a small, hairy figure ambled up beside her and then laughed when she realized it was only Bud.

"Glad you made it down safely," she told the chimp, who nodded. "Now grab ahold somewhere.

You caused this mess—the least you can do is help fix it." He drifted over beside Malik and latched onto the cloth between him and Chris, and Jules nodded. They were ready.

Or as ready as they were going to be.

The sound overhead intensified, the screech rising in pitch until it was a high, sharp tearing noise. "It's pulling free!" Mr. Enright shouted over the din. "Everyone raise the cloth up to your chin, pull it taut, and hold on tight! When the fixture falls, don't let go!"

The tearing noise suddenly stopped, and everyone gasped as the fixture tore free and dropped toward them. Jules tightened her grip and hung on as hard as she could.

Wham! The cloth tried to jerk free when the fixture hit, but Jules managed to hold on. "Take a step in!" Mr. Enright instructed. She did, as did the others, and the cloth sagged a little, the fixture dipping closer to the floor. "Now another!" The fixture was only a foot or two off the ground now, but it was no longer tugging at the cloth—it was still big, and heavy, but at least its momentum seemed to have dissipated. "One more." They all stepped closer, and with a mild, muffled thud the cloth-wrapped fixture settled onto the floor. "And you can let go." Jules had to force her hands to unclench, and she sighed in relief as the cloth dropped from her grip.

They'd done it!

"Well done, class!" Mr. Enright enthused. "An excellent job applying physics to arrest an object in motion!"

"We arrested it?" Malik joked, massaging his arms. "What were the charges?"

"Falling without a license," Tracey shot back, and they all laughed. That had been a close one!

Bud wandered over to Dr. Deere and held out a hand. The chimp was hanging his head and didn't wear his customary grin as he chittered something at the big scientist.

"That's all right," the AERIE head replied, shaking Bud's hand gently. "Accidents happen." He chuckled. "I suppose we'd better make sure our fixtures are all chimp-proof from now on!"

Bud nodded and skittered away happily, to return to Malik's side.

"Now that the excitement is over," Dr. Deere told them, "shall we continue?"

Everyone agreed. Looking at energy alternatives was going to be nice and relaxing after that!

CHAPTER 15

UP IN THE AIR

The next person they met was a short Asian man with tidy but graying hair and small, steel-framed glasses.

"Hello! Nice work with catching that fixture," he told them. "I'm Dr. Chang. I'm an aerospace engineer, and I'm in charge of our wind power program."

"Which just means you're stealing my sunlight!" Dr. Buchannan shouted from her table, much to Jules's surprise. But Dr. Chang just laughed.

"Dr. Buchannan likes to joke about that," he explained, "because wind is, ultimately, a form of solar energy—it's produced by the sun's heating our atmosphere. But people have actually been using wind power for a lot longer than they've had anything like solar cells—the earliest windmills, for example, date as far back as the Middle Ages! And we've been using wind to power ships for even longer. But James Blyth of Anderson's College in Glasgow, Scotland, built the first windmill that produced electricity, back in 1887."

A **windmill** is a building or structure with large blades, or sails, that use the force of the wind to turn and generate power.

"Fifteen years after Mouchot's solar generator," Dr. Buchannan interjected from her side of the room. "And four years after Fritts's solar cell!"

"Yes, but it was far more effective than either of those!" Dr. Chang shot back. He was smiling as he said it, though, and it was clear to Jules that the two scientists were friends who just enjoyed messing with each other. Kind of like her and her brothers.

"Dr. Buchannan is just jealous," Dr. Chang told them, "because wind power provides half of the country's renewable energy, while solar, hydroelectric, and geothermal combined make up the other half. That means I'm ahead of the game." He winked at them.

Jules raised her hand. "Why is that?" she asked. "I mean, there's always sun, and only sometimes wind, right? So why aren't we getting more power from solar cells than from windmills?"

To her relief, the scientist wasn't offended. "You're right," he agreed. "Sunlight is around more than wind, at least in some parts of the world. But as Dr. Buchannan already explained, the process to convert solar energy to electricity is a tricky one, whereas it's surprisingly easy to convert wind power to electricity. Basically the wind turns the blades, which are

131

connected to the rotor. The rotor plugs into the main shaft, which spins a generator. So as the blades turn, the turbine produces electricity. Nice and simple. Wind turbines are also very easy to build and maintain. We've got wind farms all over the country now—those are places with a whole network of big wind turbines linked together to provide electricity to entire city or county grids. But you can have smaller turbines too, for individual use. We've got ten of them spaced out along the back of the property here."

"So what are you working on, then?" Tracey asked. "It sounds like wind's already covered."

Dr. Chang laughed. "I suppose that's true, to a degree," he admitted. "But there's always room for improvement. We're looking for ways to make the wind turbines even more efficient so you can get more energy out of each one. And we're experimenting on making turbines that are stronger but also cheaper to build, so that you get more bang for your buck." He frowned for a second. "Even though the wind is free and in many places nearly constant, and wind turbines are inexpensive, we're only about 2 percent of the country's electrical power. The Department of Energy thinks we could provide as much as 20 percent of the country's electrical needs by 2030, but we've got a long way to go if we're going to get there, and every new advance helps."

"You said hydroelectric and geothermal were two other renewable energy sources," Chris pointed out. "What're those?"

Dr. Deere stepped in. "Hydroelectric power means getting electricity from water," he explained. "That's very similar to wind power, in that the water turns a turbine, which is connected to a generator. The problem is, you need a lot of water for a hydroelectric plant, and you need space to build both a dam and a reservoir so that the water can run through them with enough force to produce sufficient power. That also costs a lot of money. Of course, you can have a basic water wheel anywhere that has water with a strong enough current, but while those are great for grinding flour and other manual tasks, they don't produce a whole lot of electricity."

A **water wheel** is a machine that takes the energy of free-flowing water and turns it into usable power. A water wheel is a large metal or wooden wheel with blades or buckets set into the outer rim so that the water striking or filling those causes the wheel to turn and turns its central shaft along with it.

"And geothermal?" Malik asked. "That's like hot springs, right?"

"It is," the big scientist agreed. "Geothermal plants use Earth's natural heat as steam to turn the turbine. Those require drilling, though, just like with oil—you set it up over a geothermal reservoir and tap into it with a production well and then an injection well to return the used fluids to the reservoir again. That's a lot of work and a lot of money, just like with drilling for oil. And geothermal reservoirs can run dry too. Tapping them doesn't damage the planet, so that's a good thing, but they're still expensive and tricky to manage, which is why you don't see a lot of geothermal plants around."

Chris raised his hand. "What about nuclear power?" he asked. "That's a renewable resource, right? Because once it's up and running, it doesn't need any new resources?"

"Not exactly," Dr. Deere corrected. "Nuclear power is actually a sustainable resource. That means we can maintain it for as long as we need it. For it to be renewable, it'd have to actually replenish its resources—in this case, uranium. We need uranium to run a nuclear power plant, and we can't make new uranium, so it's not renewable. But the uranium we do have will keep us in nuclear power a long, long time."

"Does it have to be uranium?" Tracy asked. "Couldn't we use something else? Something that is renewable?"

"We're working on that," Dr. Deere admitted. "Lots of people are suggesting other options. The best one may be seawater." He laughed at their expressions. "Seriously! There's uranium in seawater— not a lot of it in terms of how much is in each liter, but when you take into account just how much seawater there is, you're talking about billions of tons of uranium. And that is a renewable resource, because uranium will keep leaking back into the seawater over time. If we can convert our nuclear plants to run on that, nuclear power would be renewable."

"Cool," Ilyana whispered. Then she shook her head. "Sounds like that's still a ways away, though."

"It is," Dr. Deere agreed, "but at least they're trying." He grinned down at the students. "We've got a couple of other tricks up our sleeves already, though. For example, check out our floor. Notice anything about it?"

Jules nodded. "It feels a little springy when you walk on it," she said. "Like the rubber mats on a playground or at a gym."

"Entirely right," Dr. Deere confirmed. "But our floor tiles are a bit more specialized than those. Because ours are kinetic floor tiles. Every time anyone walks on them, they produce electricity!"

Kinetic is a term that means of or relating to motion. Kinetic energy is the energy an object possesses because of its motion.

All of them gasped. "Whoa, really?" Tracey blurted out and then laughed at her own outburst.

But Dr. Deere clearly didn't mind. "Really," he replied. "Each step generates about four watts of power. We've got over a hundred meters of walkable surface, with roughly two hundred kinetic tiles. Even with only twenty full-time staff here, and another dozen or so part-time, we still produce a few hundred watts of power each day just from going about our business. That's basically free energy, since we'd be walking around anyway!"

"Okay, so why aren't those everywhere?" Jules asked. "Every school, every mall, every sidewalk—that would be incredible!"

"It would," Dr. Deere said. "But these tiles are still pretty expensive to produce right now. And they're thick in order to accommodate all the gears and everything inside. In order to install them in a regular floor, you'd have to actually dig down a bit first, otherwise your floor would be about three inches higher than it used to be—which doesn't sound like a lot, until you try opening a door and it can't get past the floor! We're working on ways to slim them down, though, and to lower the cost. The cheaper and flatter they get, the easier it'll be to install them in all the places you mentioned."

"Speaking of installing things," Mr. Enright called out, "I've got some exciting news." Jules realized then that their teacher had disappeared while Dr. Deere and the others were showing them around, but now he was walking back over to join them and holding up his sat phone. "I just got off the phone with Aunt Nancy," he explained, referring to his aunt, Nancy Enright, a leading inventor and businesswoman who was also the STEM class's patron, "and she agreed. We're going to give Ms. Dancy and her museum a present—we're going to make it blackout-proof!"

Everybody started talking at once. "What does that mean?" Tracey demanded. "How?" Ilyana and Chris wanted to know. "When do we start?" Malik added. And Jules chimed in with, "How can we help?"

"Whoa, whoa!" their teacher declared, throwing his hands up in mock surrender. "Slow down a second!" He was laughing, though. "To answer all your questions, what I mean is that we're going to work with Dr. Deere and the rest of AERIE to install various systems at the museum that will make sure it always has power, no matter what, and that most of its power comes from renewable resources. Aunt Nancy is putting up the money, and AERIE will be supplying the materials and the technical know-how. As far as when, we're going to start right now and do as much as we can over the course of this weekend. And yes, you can most definitely help—this is a STEM project, after all!"

"What's really amazing about all this," Dr. Deere added, "is that normally it'd take at least a year to complete a project like this. Not because the actual installations will take that long, but because usually you have to go through planning committees and budget requests and permits and all that. But since this counts as an outside donation to the museum, it can bypass a lot of that and be done right away. And since we're local, we don't even have to worry about shipping in any materials—we have everything we need right here, and we can fabricate anything else as we go." He didn't seem all that surprised by Mr. Enright's announcement, which made Jules wonder if this was something the two men had planned ahead of time, just like their class visit.

"So you're going to do it yourself?" Chris asked. "I thought you guys were mainly research."

Jules worried that Dr. Deere might take offense at that—after all, Chris had sort of just suggested that the scientists didn't know how to get their hands dirty and do the actual installation work themselves. Fortunately, the big scientist seemed amused instead. And excited!

"You're right," he agreed easily. "Usually we get called in as consultants—we point out what needs to be done and help design and build and adjust the equipment, and then we have regular technicians do the installation. But most of us here are licensed electricians, and some of us have contractor licenses as well—we build our own tools and equipment, after all, and wire them into the building so we can test them properly. It's just usually more efficient to leave the installation to someone else."

"But it'd be tough to get ahold of a qualified team on such short notice," Mr. Enright pointed out. "Especially since most technicians are probably out helping buildings recover from the blackout."

"Which is actually fine by us." Dr. Deere rubbed his hands together. "It's not often we get to go out and do the hands-on work anymore. Besides, the museum's big, but a lot smaller than, say, an airport or a mall. We can handle the job ourselves without a problem, and this way we can get started right away."

"The real question now," Mr. Enright picked up, "is what we're going to do for them." He looked at his students. "Anyone have any ideas?"

"Solar panels, obviously," Malik said first. "It's got a nice big roof, so we can put up a whole bunch of them."

Jules frowned. "We can't do kinetic tiles, can we? Not over the weekend."

"No," Dr. Deere agreed. "We'd need more time, and we'd have to rip up all the existing floors and then dig down to make space. We could look into doing that later on, maybe, but the museum also might not be happy going from marble to what looks like rubber floor tiles."

"There isn't any space for wind turbines, either," Chris said. "And no water around for hydroelectric or anything for geothermal. So solar's definitely our best bet."

Mr. Enright nodded. "I agree. But it's not just about renewable energy. What else can we do to help them prepare for blackouts?"

"Can we do anything about a water supply?" Jules asked.

"Absolutely," her teacher replied. "The museum already has gutters and drains to direct water off the roof when it rains. If we add a filtration system and a reservoir, that can actually become drinkable water. It might not be enough to take care of all the museum's needs, especially during periods of low rain, but it'll help, and there's no downside to it. What else?"

A **filtration system** is a system designed to filter impurities out of a gas or liquid.
A **reservoir** is a natural or artificial place where water is collected for use.

"Could we give them a backup generator?" Ilyana wanted to know. "That way if the power ever cut out again and the solar cells didn't have enough of a charge, they'd still have lights and heat and everything."

"We could," Mr. Enright told her, "but generators need fuel, and typically they have to go either in a basement or somewhere outside. I don't know that we want to burn oil or gas right there—we're probably better off sticking to the solar cells as much as possible."

Ilyana nodded. "What about some kind of power saver?" she asked instead. "When my computer sits for too long unused, it goes to sleep so it doesn't use as much power. If we could set up something like that for them, they'd use a lot less power."

"Like automatic lights," Malik chimed in. "That only turn on when there were people in the room. That'd save a lot of energy!"

"Good point," Mr. Enright agreed, nodding at both of them. "We can install those easily enough."

"Can we put in some kind of emergency lighting?" Tracey asked, and Jules knew her friend was thinking about how they'd all stood around in the dark last night. "That only turns on when the power goes out?"

"Certainly," Mr. Enright said. "We could put them along the halls, in the exhibit rooms, and in the bathrooms and offices. They wouldn't need to be big, just enough to find the walls and the doors. They'd probably need to be battery powered, but that's fine, since they'd only come on when the power went out."

Jules rubbed her hands together. This was going to be so cool! She couldn't wait to see the look on Ms. Dancy's face when they told her what they were going to do for her museum and the look on her face when it was all finished!

CHAPTER 16

STAYING IN POWER

Dr. Deere turned and started shouting out orders to the rest of his team. At the same time, he was typing on a tablet and muttering to himself, things like, "Right, so we'll need at least two hundred feet of cable, better grab extra, and . . ."

Malik hated to interrupt when it was clear that the AERIE's lead scientist was so busy, but a question was eating away at him. "Dr. Deere?" he asked tentatively.

The big scientist glanced up. "Hmm?" He didn't seem annoyed, though, so Malik pressed on.

"Sorry, I know you're busy," he started, "but I've got a question."

Much to his surprise, Dr. Deere immediately set down the tablet and gave Malik his full attention. "Ask away," he said with a smile. That smile only broadened at the surprise Malik was sure showed on his own face. "There's nothing more important than education," the big scientist explained. "And if you've got something important you want to know, then that's important to the rest of us."

The rest of his class had stopped what they were doing as well, as had Mr. Enright and even the other scientists. Malik felt like he was under a spotlight—or a microscope—and for a second he worried that he was simply wasting everyone's time. But fortunately his natural outgoingness won out over his nervousness. Or, as his mom liked to say, "Malik's never met an audience he didn't like." So he gathered up his courage and continued.

"I was just wondering," he said, forcing himself to stand up straight and speak slowly and clearly. "I mean, all of this"—he waved his hand at the research institute—"it's killer stuff. Solar panels, wind turbines, kinetic tiles, water wheels, the works. So if we've got all this amazing technology, all these ways to use renewable energy, why aren't we? Dr. Chang said wind could be covering as much as 20 percent of the country's energy needs by 2030, and earlier he said that wind power was about half of the country's renewable energy. But that means that, if the others grow at the same rate, by 2030 we'll still only be relying on renewable energy for 40 percent of our energy. Which means 60 percent is still going to come from oil and gas and coal. Right?"

Dr. Deere nodded. He didn't look happy, but Malik could tell that wasn't directed at him. "Your numbers are spot-on," the big scientist told him. "And a lot of people think the Department of Energy is being overly optimistic, that we won't be able to cover anywhere near that 20 percent, not even by then." He rubbed at his face, making his bushy black mustache stick out like an enraged caterpillar. "So yes, that's a really good question. We have the technology, sure. Even without some of the advances we're working on here, there's no reason why solar panels and wind farms couldn't provide energy for more than half of our electrical needs right now. So why aren't we?"

Mr. Enright stepped in. "It *is* a really good question," he agreed, which made Malik proud. "Anybody have any ideas for an answer? Why aren't we using a lot more renewable energy already?"

They all stopped to think about that for a bit. "Is it because it's easier to stick with what you know?" Tracey asked after a minute. "And wouldn't the existing power companies have to change everything around in order to start using solar panels and other renewable resources? That's a lot of work, right?"

"It certainly is," their teacher answered. "And smaller, newer companies could come along and scoop up some of the business because they can just start with solar panels, rather than having to alter all their equipment and training and facilities. So the big companies aren't eager to take that risk. What else?"

This time Chris spoke up. "You said wind turbines aren't all that expensive, and they're easy to put up and easy to maintain," he said to Dr. Chang, who nodded. "So if we had all these wind farms all over the country, they wouldn't need a whole lot of maintenance, right? But power plants now have a ton of people working for them—one of my neighbors works at one, and he's always talking about how crowded it is, how there's never room in the parking lot or in the cafeteria because they've got so many workers there. So if we switched to wind farms and solar panels, a lot of those people would lose their jobs. I bet all of them would vote for sticking with oil and gas and coal just for that reason."

"Plus with solar panels," Jules chimed in, "you don't even need a power company, do you? You put them on your roof and they feed right into your house. Same if you've got your own wind turbine in your backyard. So the power companies aren't supplying you with power anymore, which means they're losing money too."

"All accurate," Mr. Enright confirmed. "The power companies aren't entirely thrilled with the idea of renewable energy. They'd be fine with it if switching over meant that they would still make as much money, and could still employ as many workers, but that's not the case. And if it were the case, there wouldn't be as much reason to switch—renewable power is good for the environment, yes, but it's also cheaper to use and cheaper to maintain, and that's part of the appeal."

"It's not all cheap, though, is it?" Malik asked. "You said hydroelectric power is expensive, at least at the start, because you've got to build a dam and set up a reservoir. And geothermal plants need to have wells drilled, so that's expensive too. It's like when we redid all the plumbing in our house last year—it was expensive to do, but my dad said once it was done we'd save money because it was more efficient now." He snickered a little, remembering. "He wasn't too happy about shelling out the money to start, though!"

The adults all laughed at that. "That's an excellent point," Mr. Enright said after a minute. "And yes, that's been a big factor in people's resistance. Switching to renewable resources will involve a great deal of time and money to make the change. Once it's done, we'll have cheaper, cleaner, safer energy, and we won't be wrecking the environment, but there's that initial expense—and that's a tough one for a lot of people to swallow. They figure everything's working fine now, so why change it?"

"But it's not working!" Ilyana burst out. "That's why we're having a blackout right now! Because we're using too much energy, and we're not producing enough, and we're killing the planet in the process!"

"Absolutely," Dr. Deere agreed. "And, fortunately, more and more people are starting to realize that. The federal government has been paying a lot more attention these past few years. They've done studies on clean, renewable energy; they've set up more solar panels and more wind farms, and they're looking into other options. Part of our funding comes from a government grant. And more and more people are realizing how dangerous and expensive nonrenewable energy is. Lots of people are buying solar panels for their homes. Farms and other rural buildings are putting up wind turbines too. We're getting there." He sighed. "It's a slow process, but we're starting to get people to realize how important this is. And what a big difference it could make for our country, and the rest of the world, moving forward."

"And the cheaper and easier and stronger you make things like solar panels and wind turbines," Tracey said, "the more people will come around, right?"

Dr. Deere laughed. "Right! Like Dr. Buchannan said, we want to make these things so inexpensive and so effective that people would be fools *not* to want them!" He stroked his mustache. "It's just like with smartphones, really. When the first mobile phones came out, they were big and bulky and awkward and didn't stay powered up for very long. The only people who had them were people who really needed them or people who wanted to show off. But as cell phones got smaller and cheaper, more and more people started using them—and as they added more and more functions, more and more people started wanting them. These days, pretty much everybody has a cell phone, and people look at you funny if you don't because they're so useful and so inexpensive that nobody can figure out why you wouldn't have one. We want to do the same for renewable energy."

"And one way to do that," Mr. Enright added, "is to install renewable power sources in public places so that everyone can see how impressive they are and how much they help." He smiled. "Just like we're going to do for the museum."

"Exactly," Dr. Deere agreed. "We do a lot of projects with malls and sports arenas and schools for that precise reason. They're really visible, so everyone who passes through those can see just how effective these new options are. Some airports have kinetic tiles in their halls now, for example, and those power the lights along those halls. It's a great way to use the constant traffic they get, and everyone who passes through there sees the little plaque explaining that their own footsteps are what's keeping the lights on."

Ilyana had a question. "Wouldn't it be a good idea to focus on places that really need to have power no matter what?" she asked. "I mean, solar panels in a school or a mall is sick, but what about a hospital? What do they do when the power goes out?"

"You're correct," their teacher told her. "It's super important for hospitals to maintain power. A lot of their patients need medical equipment just to stay alive, and those all run on electricity. And if the power goes out during a surgery, that can put the patient at risk too. That's why most hospitals have backup generators, so that if the city loses power they can keep running for at least a little longer on their own. But a lot more hospitals are adding solar panels, either instead of those old generators or as a way to supplement them. The government knows how important medical services are, so they're putting a lot of emphasis on making sure hospitals have the resources they need to keep functioning even during a major crisis—and that includes blackouts."

Everyone breathed a sigh of relief hearing that, including Malik. It was good to know the government was taking the energy problem seriously.

Then Dr. Deere grinned and clapped his hands together. "Enough serious talk!" he boomed. "Let's go see about turning the lights back on at your museum, hey?"

Malik's entire class clapped and cheered.

CHAPTER 17

UNDER THE WEATHER

"Good thing we've got nice weather today," one of the AERIE researchers, a woman named Linda Marx, commented as Jules helped her lug a pile ·of cables out to the bus. "This would be a whole lot harder if the weather had turned against us."

"I can imagine," Jules replied, shivering at the thought of carrying all these supplies back and forth in the rain or, worse, snow. The adults had decided to send some of the new equipment and gear on ahead in the STEM bus, since they had extra space and were going back to the museum anyway. Dr. Deere and the rest of the AERIE team would follow in their own vans, along with the rest of their supplies and materials.

"Oh, it's not just because carrying everything in the rain would be no fun," Linda told her as they passed the cables to Randall, who was arranging them in the back of the bus and turned to head back inside for more. "Right now we've only got to deal with the issue of not having any power at the museum. But

bad weather can add all sorts of other problems to the equation."

"Like what?" Tracey asked. She and Ilyana were hauling a box full of components, and Malik and Chris were right behind them with another.

Linda frowned as the STEM kids all gathered around her. "Well," she started, "think about it.

Imagine if it were winter—real winter, not the kind you get here, but with ice and snow and freezing cold. Think about what that'd be like without any power."

"Everything would freeze because you wouldn't have any heat," Chris guessed. "Though at least you wouldn't have to worry about your food spoiling!"

"True," Mr. Enright agreed, having snuck up behind them during the conversation. He had a large toolbox in each hand. "In fact, back before the wonders of modern refrigeration, people in northern climates used to preserve their food by burying it in the ice and snow, or by tying a sturdy rope around it and lowering it into the frozen river. Food would keep all winter long like that, without any help. You just had to remember to haul it back up or dig it back out and eat it once the thaw hit!"

"Sure, the food'd be fine, but you'd freeze to death!" Tracey argued. "That doesn't sound like a very good trade-off to me!"

"You could light a fire," Malik shot back. "And you could bundle up, add lots of layers. But you're right, I wouldn't want to go through a real winter without heat!"

"And what would that do to all your wiring and plumbing?" their teacher pointed out. "Did you know that every winter in New Orleans they warn people not to defrost frozen pipes with blowtorches? Because the houses down there are all raised off the ground, since it floods so easily, which means the pipes under the houses are all exposed. That's great if you're trying to get in to work on a broken pipe, but the few times it gets cold enough, all the pipes freeze. And there are always people who figure they'll just crawl under their house and thaw the pipes out themselves—using a blowtorch." He shook his head. "You can imagine how well that works out!"

"Why don't they insulate their pipes properly?" Jules asked. "That way they wouldn't freeze."

Insulate means to protect something from losing heat—or shield it from sound—by wrapping it in other materials.

"Because it doesn't happen that often," Mr. Enright replied. "So they figure it's an extra expense they won't really need."

"Can your wiring freeze too?" Ilyana wanted to know. "Because if that happened, you'd have a really hard time getting the power back on, wouldn't you?"

"You would," Linda agreed. "It's a lot harder for wiring to freeze than for pipes, since the pipes have water in them and that can turn to ice as soon as the temperature dips below freezing, but it can happen. What's more likely is that ice will form on some of the outside connectors, like the ones leading from the transformers to your fuse box. If that happens, it'll break the connection, and even if the electricity comes back on, you might still be without power. Or it could create a spark, which can cause a fire or make your whole system short circuit."

"Then there's the issue of thunderstorms," Mr. Enright added. "That's a common cause of blackouts, when lightning hits a transformer and shorts it out, taking out an entire city grid. But that lightning strike causes a power surge—it's actually a good thing if it blows the transformer, because otherwise it'll send that extra energy down the line and into homes and buildings along the way. That can fry every electrical device in your house. I've even heard of computers and toasters and microwaves melting from the excess electricity!"

A **transformer** is a device that conducts electricity and controls the voltage traveling from one circuit to another.

"Melting? Really?" Jules asked, but their teacher nodded.

"Really. And that can start fires too, of course. That's why, when there's a major thunderstorm, you should get off your computer, turn off your TV, and shut down and disconnect as many electrical devices as you can. You don't want to take that risk."

"And use surge protectors," Linda added. "Always have a surge protector on your computer. A lot of extension cords have built-in surge protectors these days, which is a big help. That way if there is a sudden surge through the lines, the surge protector will short itself out and block the charge from reaching and damaging your electronics. Better to have to replace a power cord than your whole computer or TV!"

"Is that what's going on with the blackout now?" Jules asked. "Is there a risk of everything overloading?"

"Actually, no," Linda told her. "The current blackouts and brownouts are deliberate this time."

"Deliberate?" Ilyana asked. "You mean somebody's causing all these power outages? Is it a super-villain who's out to rob the city or something?"

Jules rolled her eyes and shared a chuckle with Tracey. Ilyana loved books and movies, but sometimes she got a little carried away and forgot what was fiction and what was real life.

Mr. Enright was laughing as well, but not meanly. "No, it's actually the city that's causing these blackouts," he explained, "and there's nothing sinister about them. People are using too much electricity at the moment, that's all. They're putting a strain on the system. The city's tried asking people to tamp down their personal usage but hardly anyone's listening— we're all so used to the idea of being able to flick a switch any time we like that we're not willing to do without. City officials are worried that the grid might overload, and that could be devastating—lots of important systems could shut down, there could be plenty of damage both to the city and to private homes and buildings, and it would take a great deal of time and money to fix. So, in order to take some of the pressure off the system, they've instituted a system of rolling brownouts and blackouts."

Malik snapped his fingers. "It's like going on a diet!" he declared. "You can't tell somebody to stop eating because they'll just get hungry and gorge themselves. Instead, you tell them to cut back a little, maybe have one cookie instead of two, so they can build up to it gradually. Or you keep them so busy they miss lunch one day, or tell them to skip a snack the next day. They get used to the idea of eating a little less, and eventually, even when they've got access to all the food they want, they've learned to eat only when they're actually hungry." He shrugged at the funny looks the others were giving him. "My uncle's been trying to lose weight for years," he explained sheepishly, "and he likes to talk about all the different things he's tried, but the one that finally worked was simply training himself to stop when he was full instead of eating just because there was still food in front of him."

Mr. Enright clapped a hand on Malik's shoulder.

"That's a great analogy, Malik," their teacher said, "and you're spot on. The city's hoping that, in addition to easing the pressure on the system by shutting down power here and there for short periods of time, having no power will make people a little more cautious about overusing it. We don't really need to have every light on in our house, and the TV, and the stereo, and our computer, do we? We can just have the light on in whatever room we're in, and turn on whichever device we're using at the time. If we could get everyone to do that, we could cut our power usage in half or more, which means we'd need a lot less power to keep everyone happy."

"Or we can give everyone solar panels and wind turbines and kinetic tiles and all that," Chris suggested, "and then they can use as much power as they want, because they're not drawing from the city's power grid at all."

"Sure," Jules agreed, "and if that's their only source of power, and it suddenly cuts out because they've used too much of it, they'd have to learn how to ration it better! It'd be like those diets where you only get so much food each day, so if you pig out first thing in the morning, you'll wind up hungry that night, but by the third or fourth day you'll realize that you've got to eat only a little for breakfast and save the rest for lunch and dinner."

But Malik was shaking his head. "I sure hope that works better with electrical usage than it does with food," he declared, "because if my Uncle Aban is any example, he'll just stuff himself every morning and spend the whole rest of the day moaning about how hungry he is and wondering why there isn't any food left!"

They all laughed and turned back to collect more supplies. Jules hoped Malik was right, though, about rationing working better with power than with food. It was a terrible thought that people couldn't learn how to control themselves and restrict their usage to what was really important, especially if that meant that everyone, both those people and the ones who really didn't overuse electricity anyway, wound up suffering because of it.

"Don't worry," Mr. Enright told her, as if he could read her mind. "The brownouts and blackouts are helping. And they really do make some people wake up and realize they've got to be more careful. Many of them learn to make do with a little less. But others are looking into things like solar panels and wind turbines, just as Chris said. And for every person who starts relying upon renewable energy, the grid has an easier time supporting the needs of everyone else."

Jules nodded. She just hoped it would be enough.

CHAPTER 18

GOING OFF THE GRID

The drive back to the museum was a lot less eventful than the drive to AERIE had been. They did see several police out directing traffic, and each one gave their bus a curious glance, clearly wondering why a school bus would be out during a blackout, especially on a Saturday. But no one tried to stop them. Not that Malik was too worried—Mr. Enright had talked them out of trouble the first time around, so there was no reason he couldn't do it again—but it was probably better this way.

When they pulled up outside the museum, Ms. Dancy was waiting for them, along with two policemen who had clearly been sent to provide the extra security Dr. Pillai had mentioned. "Thank you so much for arranging all this!" Ms. Dancy told Mr. Enright. "When your aunt called, well, I was just stunned! And the thought that people will be able to enjoy our exhibits without having to worry about power outages is wonderful!" She beamed at him, and at the class. "Plus the idea that a natural history museum, which teaches all about the past, will now also show the way to the future! The irony is breathtaking!"

Irony is when a situation is deliberately the opposite of what you'd expect, or when you deliberately use words to signify the opposite of what they would normally mean.

"You're very welcome," Mr. Enright assured her. Then he introduced Dr. Deere, Dr. Buchannan, and the other specialists.

"I think we should install the solar panels first," Dr. Buchannan suggested. She peered up at the sky. "We've got good visibility right now, plenty of sunlight," she pointed out, "and it hasn't rained lately so the roof will be dry. If we wait too long we'll have to use lanterns and searchlights just so we can see what we're doing, which will make it a whole lot more dangerous. Plus, if we can get the panels up before the sun goes down, they can start building a charge right away."

Dr. Deere nodded. "Good plan," he agreed. "You take your team and get started up there. I'll check out the museum's electrical systems to make sure they'll be up to the task."

"Where do you want us?" Tracey asked.

The big scientist started to reply, and Malik could see from his expression that the man was going to tell them to go back to class and stay out of the way. "This is a STEM project," he pointed out, cutting Dr. Deere off before he could speak. "Which means we should be involved. And we can help. We're good at this kind of hands-on stuff—it's what STEM's for. Right, Mr. Enright?"

"Absolutely," their teacher answered. He frowned at Dr. Deere. "You wouldn't be trying to sideline my kids, would you, Don?" But then he laughed. "Because you know that's not happening! We're in it, so you'd better tell us what to do before we just start picking our own assignments!"

"All right, all right!" Dr. Deere threw up his hands. "I know better than to argue with you, Todd! Why don't you kids help Dr. Buchannan and her team install the solar panels—if you're okay with being up there."

"Up on the roof?" Malik gulped a little at the thought but put on a brave face. "Sure, we can handle it!" After all, they'd faced a flash flood, and they'd climbed onto the roof of a house back then. How much worse could this be? At least it wasn't raining!

The others all nodded too. Malik thought Ilyana looked a little green at the idea, but clearly none of them were willing to be left out.

Randall, of course, was all for the idea. "Yes! High-altitude ops!" he declared, pumping his fist.

Malik tried not to roll his eyes but wound up laughing instead because Bud was mimicking Randall, pumping his own hairy little fist while jumping up and down and hooting. At least the chimp would be comfortable with heights, Malik figured.

"Everybody ready?" Dr. Buchannan asked. Once the class had all said they were, she led them and her own assistants into the museum's front lobby. From there, however, they immediately turned off and took a narrow set of stairs up to the second floor, which was all offices and utilities and storage rooms. Ms. Dancy had come with them, and she showed the way down one hall to a ceiling hatch at the far end. A metal ladder was permanently bolted into the wall just below it.

"Good luck," the museum curator said as one of the AERIE techs took the lead, quickly climbing the ladder and wrestling the hatch open before pulling himself up and through. A minute later he was leaning back into the opening, gesturing, and someone else handed up one of the spools of cable. Once most of the gear had been passed up, the rest of them climbed up to join him.

The good news was, the museum had a wide, flat roof, and it was stone like the rest of the building. There was even a wide lip around the edge! Malik was a lot more comfortable standing up there than he'd expected, and looking around he thought his friends felt the same way.

Dr. Buchannan was glancing around as well. "This should make things a lot easier," she declared as she surveyed the rooftop. "Okay, let's break out the chalk lines and grid it out."

"What does that mean?" Chris asked. They all watched as the techs pulled out teardrop-shaped yellow-and-black plastic devices with crank-style handles mounted on top.

"These are chalk lines," the solar panel expert explained, holding up the one in her hand. "Basically I hand someone this"—she offered it to Malik, who took it—"and you hold it down on the rooftop, completely steady, while I take this part"—she pulled a small metal tab at the narrower end and it came free, revealing that it was attached to a long cord—"and walk all the way down here." Dr. Buchannan walked to the other end of the roof, staying in a straight line as far as Malik could tell. When she reached the far side, she turned around and squatted down, holding the metal tab just above the ground. "Turn the handle on the top," she called back, and Malik grabbed the handle and began turning it. As he did, the chalk line tightened, until it was nice and taut. Dr. Buchannan pressed the tab to the roof, holding it there a few seconds before she lifted it up and rose to her feet once more. "Now lift your end and carry it four paces to your left," she instructed. Malik did so, and she kept pace with him. When he'd gone four paces, she indicated that he should set the tool on the ground again, and again she knelt down and pressed the metal tab to the ground.

"Check it out!" Ilyana whispered, pointing. Sure enough, where the line had been, there was now a blue line stretching all the way across the roof. Another line marked their first position.

"Solar panels get mounted four feet apart," Dr. Buchannan explained from the other end. "That's about four full paces for someone with size ten to eleven shoes, and I'm guessing that's about what you wear." It was—Malik might not be all that tall yet, but his dad kept telling him he had the feet of a larger man and just needed to grow into them. "Once we lay out the lines along this axis, two others can mark lines going perpendicular, and that way we'll wind up with a perfect grid showing exactly where we need to mount our solar panels. Got it?" Malik nodded, and she rewarded him with a smile. "Great! Then let's get moving!"

Perpendicular is when two objects or lines exist at right angles (ninety degrees) from each other.
Parallel is when two objects or lines run even to one another, always the same distance apart and never touching or meeting.

Once the grid was done, Dr. Buchannan explained their next step. "We need to set up our mounts," she told them, pointing to the collection of metal rods and slats piled up off to one side. "There are two types of roof mounts for solar panels: ballasted and nonballasted. A ballasted system relies on weight to keep the panels in place. You don't actually need to attach anything; you just set up the mounting systems, fasten your panels to them, and you're all set."

A **ballast** is a heavy material that is added near the bottom of a ship or other vessel to give it increased stability.

"But what if there's a lot of wind?" Jules asked. "Wouldn't they just blow away?"

"Precisely!" Dr. Buchannan answered. "I don't like ballasted systems for that exact reason. They're great if you can't risk drilling into the roof—like it's all tile or something else that could shatter easily—but, yes, if the area has high winds the whole system could get destroyed. Nonballasted systems are where you actually drill in and attach the mounting system directly to the roof. It's a lot sturdier, and a lot more stable, but some people worry about roof damage." She shrugged. "That's not going to be an issue here, so we're attaching ours."

She showed them how to assemble one of the mounts. They were made so you could adjust their angle when you put them together. "You need to know what angle to tilt your mounts at," she told them, "because otherwise you'll either bounce the sunlight back up into the sky or send it somewhere they don't use it properly, or scatter it off to the side where it won't do any good."

"How do you figure out the angle?" Malik asked. Who knew that putting in solar panels would be so reliant on math!

"It's based on your latitude," the researcher answered. "You start out tilting them by twenty-five degrees, then add another five degrees for every five we're past twenty-five degrees latitude." Pulling out her smartphone, Dr. Buchannan did something. "We're at almost exactly thirty-four degrees north," she announced. "That means we're looking at a tilt of twenty-five degrees plus just about ten more, or thirty-five degrees in all." She demonstrated how to adjust the angle, and the kids got to work assembling and adjusting the mounts she'd assigned them. Her assistants were already hard at work setting up the rest.

Latitude is the distance north or south from the earth's equator, measured in degrees and minutes.

"This is pretty easy," Chris commented to Malik as they worked on one together. "Now that she showed us how, I mean."

"Yeah, I wouldn't want to have to figure all that out on my own," Malik replied, "but you're right, it's simple enough now."

"Come on, slowpokes!" Randall was shouting at them. He was at one end, right by the lip, and had a finished mount in his hands. "Look, this is how it's done, see?" Holding the mount over his head, he spun in a circle. But just as he was half turned, a breeze caught the mount and tugged at it, and at him, sending Randall staggering to one side—and right toward the lip, and the long fall to the ground beyond!

Just as Randall bumped into the lip and toppled over it, a small, hairy hand shot out from behind him and grabbed the mount. It yanked hard, tugging the device back toward the rest of them. And since Randall was still clutching onto the mount for dear life, he was pulled along as well, sprawling onto the roof in front of them, bruised and a little scraped but at least out of harm's way. For now.

"Nice save, Bud!" Malik called out, and his pal grinned, showing all his teeth. Because, sure enough, it had been the former NASA chimp who had dragged Randall back to safety.

"Saved by a chimp . . . again," Chris muttered under his breath, referring back to Randall's escapades during the flash flood. "That's gotta be embarrassing!"

He and Malik laughed. Randall did look a little red in the face as he hopped back to his feet and stormed off to help some of the techs finish marking along each

grid line where the mounts would go. Malik did feel a little bad for their teacher's aide, but the guy kept bringing it upon himself. After all, who danced around on a rooftop waving a big metal frame over his head? That was just asking for trouble!

"These look great," Dr. Buchannan told them all as she inspected the finished mounts. "Now we need to fasten them to the roof. You have to drill each hole first, then clean out the hole and install the anchor. We still use the old-fashioned method of tapping them in with a hammer to make sure each anchor's nice and secure. Once those are in place, we set up the mounts and screw the bolts into their anchors, and we're all set." She showed them one, then offered up the drill—which Malik noticed was battery-powered. "Who wants to try?"

Each of the kids took a turn drilling. It was stressful, Malik found when he got to try, mainly because he didn't want to screw anything up. Plus, the drill shook in his hand, and he had to grip it tightly to keep it from shaking loose. By contrast, tapping the anchor into place was easy; it just required a steady hand.

With so many of them working on the project at once, it didn't take them long to drill all of the holes, insert all of the anchors, set the mounts in place, and bolt them down.

"Now for the easy part," Dr. Buchannan assured them. "The panels have a built-in mount interface, so we just have to set them on the mounts and make sure they click into place, and they're all set." She gestured at the first finished one. "Notice that it's six inches off the surface," she pointed out. "That's to allow proper airflow around the panel. They work better when there's more circulation."

"And the cables?" Jules asked, pointing to the wires running from each panel. "Those run to a battery, right? To store the current until it's needed?"

"That's right," the solar panel scientist confirmed. She rubbed her hands together and then wiped them on her jeans. "We're all set up here, so provided that Dr. Deere's got the wiring in place down below, our job is done." She gestured back toward the roof hatch. "After you."

"Hey, Randall," Malik couldn't resist calling out as they traipsed back toward the hatch and its ladder, "maybe you should let Bud go first. Just in case."

"Ha, ha," their teacher's aide called back. But when the chimp pushed past him, he didn't argue.

CHAPTER 19

CROSSED WIRES

"We've got the filtration system in place," one of the AERIE researchers was reporting to Dr. Deere when Jules and her classmates made it back down to the museum's main floor. "And we've rerouted the gutters so the water'll flow through that and then into the existing tanks, so that's all set."

A **gutter** is a shallow groove just below the edge of a roof that is used to carry off rainwater.

"Nice," the big AERIE head said, clapping the researcher on the shoulder. Then he glanced over and saw the STEM kids. "Ah, and how'd it go on the roof?" he asked. "Solar panels all set?"

"Yep," Jules confirmed with a smile. "Dr. Buchannan said it's all done up there."

"It is indeed," the solar panel scientist called out from behind them as she and her team hurried to catch up. "They did a great job." She spared a sharp glance for Randall. "Even if one or two were monkeying around a bit too much."

"And one was monkeying around just enough!" Malik added, patting Bud on the head. The chimp nodded, bouncing on his feet the way he often did when he was excited, and they all laughed—all except Randall, who was still a bit red in the face. Jules felt a little sorry for him, actually, but it had been his own fault, and if the worst consequence was that they teased him for a bit, well, there were worse fates.

"Great," Dr. Deere was saying when she returned her attention to him. "We've got the wiring in place, so we'll plug that into the solar panels and that's another system installed." He flicked a glance toward his watch and beamed. "And ahead of schedule, too! Nice having so many helpful hands!"

"What's next?" Chris wanted to know. Jules and the others nodded. Getting to help upgrade the museum was epic. This was what she loved about STEM, that they didn't just talk about science and math and all that—they actually got to apply them to real-world problems and then have a hand in fixing them!

Dr. Deere pondered for a moment. "Well, we're about to put in the emergency lights," he replied. "You could help install those."

He led them over to the side, where one of the other techs was crouched down by a wall outlet. It was Linda Marx. "Hey, kids," she greeted them as they gathered around her. She had a screwdriver in her hand and what looked like a night-light sitting in an opened carton on the floor beside her.

"Want some help?" Ilyana asked.

"I wouldn't say no," the researcher replied. "This isn't hard, but it takes time, and we've got a bunch to do, so if we divide and conquer that'd be great."

"Those are the emergency lights?" Tracey asked, gesturing at the carton. "And you just plug them in?"

"Well, not quite." Linda lifted the light out of its packaging. "First, you check to make sure it's working—it's got batteries already installed, so you just need to pull the little plastic tab free so they can function. Do that and then hit the manual 'on' switch here to test them." She showed them where the switch was and flicked it, and the light came on. It wasn't terribly bright, but Jules figured it didn't have to be—it would be enough to give a faint glow around it, which would allow people to see where they were going along an otherwise dark hall.

"Works fine," the researcher remarked, "so turn it back off"—which she did—"and then attach it."

Jules had another question. "Some plugs have three prongs," she pointed out, "but others, like this one, only have two. What's the difference?"

"The third prong acts as a ground," Linda explained. "It's to keep you from getting electrocuted in case a strong charge builds up in the device. These lights don't actually draw any electricity, since they're designed so they only turn on when the power goes out—they're just measuring the power from the outlet and using its absence to know when they have to switch on. So they shouldn't ever be building a charge at all, which is why they don't need the ground. All we have to do is plug them in"—she demonstrated—"and voilà!" The light immediately switched on.

"How do we know it's working correctly, though?" Tracey asked. "I mean, it's on now, but how do we know it'll turn on every time the power cuts out?"

"And turn off when the power comes back on," Chris added. He shrugged. "Otherwise its batteries'll burn out really fast, right?"

"They would," Linda agreed. She frowned. "You're right; we need to be sure. Okay, come with me." She unplugged the light and, cradling it carefully, got back to her feet. Then she led them through the lobby and outside to one of the AERIE vans.

"We keep equipment to test things with," she told them as she opened the back of the van, rummaged through the bins built in along its sides, and finally pulled something out. "Aha!" What she held looked like someone had literally cut a section out of a wall, complete with the outlet. But on the back, instead of loose wiring, was a large battery, the kind you'd find in a heavy-duty lantern. "This lets us test things by plugging them in and switching the power on and off," Linda explained. She plugged the light into the outlet and it turned on again. Then she flipped the switch and the light turned off. When she flipped the switch again, the light came back on. "Looks good," she declared.

"The light, yeah," someone commented, and they all glanced over to see Mr. Enright approaching them, with Dr. Deere at his side. "But we do have a problem."

Dr. Deere was holding a device in his hand, and Jules recognized it. "That's a multimeter!" she said, earning her a surprised look from her classmates. "It's what our old neighbor used to check our wiring the other day," she reminded them. "I told you guys about that."

"It is," Dr. Deere confirmed, "and unfortunately its readings aren't great." He held up the multimeter, and Jules saw that the little digital readout said 112.3.

"That's low, isn't it?" she asked. "Mr. Negavi said it should be right around 120."

"It should be," the big scientist agreed. "A little fluctuation's fine, but it should really be within two or three points of that number. This is lower." He nodded to Linda. "Reset the outlet there so it's only putting out 110."

She turned the panel around and fiddled with a knob beside the battery. "Got it." Then she flipped the switch. The light stayed on. "Uh-oh."

"Exactly," Dr. Deere sighed.

"What does that mean?" Chris asked. "That the lights will stay on even when the power's back up?"

"Probably so," Mr. Enright confirmed. "The problem is that the museum's wiring is too old. It's not maintaining a proper current. And these emergency lights are so sensitive that they'll register that lower current as not being sufficient power, so they'll kick on. And stay on."

"Can we replace the wiring?" Tracey asked. But both scientists as well as Mr. Enright shook their heads.

"That's a lot of extra work," their teacher answered, "and a lot more money, and a whole lot of time. It can be done, of course, and it really should be at some point soon, but there's no way we can do that right now."

"So we have to ditch the emergency lights?" Jules asked. She hated the idea of people having to stumble around in the dark, even if that wasn't likely to happen as much now that they'd added the solar panels.

"We might," Mr. Enright agreed. Then he gave them a mischievous look. "Unless you can think of a way to fix them."

That was a clear challenge, and Jules and her friends huddled together to come up with ideas.

"We could use the manual switches," Ilyana suggested. "But that would mean somebody going along and flipping each one whenever the lights went out, and then going back and turning them all back off after." She frowned. "That's a whole lot of work, and if they're doing that, they can just have flashlights or lanterns or whatever."

Malik perked up. "Hey, my backyard light turns on when it gets dark out," he told them. "It's got some kind of light sensor that tells it when that happens. And then when the sun comes back up, it turns back off—or if we pull up and the headlights catch it just right. Maybe we could do something like that here?"

The kids turned back to the adults, who had been listening in. "That would work," Dr. Deere agreed slowly, rubbing his chin. "We've got light sensors—we'd have to wire them into each emergency light, but it's just a matter of cracking open the case, taking out the power gauges, connecting the light sensors, cutting a small hole in the side of the casing for the wires, closing them back up, and then gluing the sensors to the case exterior."

A **gauge** is an instrument or device used to measure something, typically energy or fluid.

"Oh, is that all?" Tracey muttered. "Sure. Maybe we can just go ahead and rewire the building while we're at it!" Jules grinned at her. She knew her friend was just grousing, mainly because Tracey was used to working on cars—she'd said more than once that every time something looked like a small, easy fix it wound up being part of something much bigger that took a whole lot longer.

But Linda laughed. "It sounds like a lot of work," she admitted, "but it's really not that bad. We could probably fix each light in a few minutes, especially if we do it like an assembly line, with each person handling a single task. So one person opens the cases, another follows behind and snips the wires, a third pulls the power gauge, a fourth connects the sensor wires, a fifth cuts the hole and closes the case, and a sixth glues the sensors on."

"There're five of us," Jules declared, "six with Randall." The teacher's aide nodded enthusiastically— it looked like he was as eager to help as they were! "So we could do that, if you show us how."

"My pleasure." The researcher dug around in the bins for a minute and came up with a handful of supplies. "Here, watch this."

She showed them how to modify the lights step by step, explaining as she went. It really did look easy, and it only took her a few minutes just as she'd said, but Jules knew that was partially because Linda was an expert. They weren't. Still, she thought they could handle it.

"Let's get all the lights and lay them out in the main hall," Linda said once she'd finished that light and tested it—it worked perfectly, turning on when it was dark and off when there was light, regardless of whether the outlet had power. "I'll get each of you set up with your task, and then I'll circle around and check to make sure you've got it right, plus I'll be there if you have any questions or if there's any trouble."

That made Jules feel a lot better. Linda was nice, and clearly good at her job, so with her there, Jules was sure they could handle the task.

Dr. Deere evidently thought so as well. "I can see this project's in good hands," he told them, clapping his own enormous hands together. "So I'll leave you to it while I make sure those solar panels are plugged in." He turned and headed back inside.

"I've got a few other things to check on, myself," Mr. Enright declared. He smiled at them. "Don't worry, I'll be back soon. I expect to find the whole building lit up by the time I return."

Jules and the others watched him go and then gave Linda their full attention. "Okay," Jules told the woman, "show us what to do."

CHAPTER 20

THINGS HEAT UP

I t took a little time, but eventually the kids all got into a certain rhythm. Randall was responsible for cracking open each case. Ilyana was behind him with the wire cutters, snipping the wires that connected the power gauges to the lights themselves. Then Jules pulled out the power gauges. Chris connected the sensor wires, and Tracey—who was the most experienced of them when it came to tools—drilled a tiny hole in the casing and shut it, making sure the wires had space to pass through the hole. Finally, Malik glued the sensors to the top of the case, where they'd be able to catch the most light.

Malik found that he enjoyed having the last task in the assembly line. It was like he was the finishing crew, putting the final touch on each piece. Linda Marx was right behind him to check each light as he did, and to pronounce them done. Once all the lights had been adjusted, she picked several at random to try out in the AERIE test panel. They all worked just fine. "We

could try each one," she told them, "but that would take even longer. I watched all of you working, and I didn't see any mistakes, and each one we've tried has worked just fine, so they should all be good."

The kids all cheered and high-fived each other. It was really excellent to be part of all this, and to be able to check yet another step in the museum's renovation off their list.

Just then, Mr. Enright reappeared. "All done?" he asked. "Splendid! And perfect timing. Remember I said I had some things to check on? Well, I've got a surprise for you all. Follow me!"

"Don't worry about the lights," Linda assured them. "I'll gather a few of the other techs and we'll take care of putting them in the spots we'd marked out on the map." Malik knew that there would be a few lights spaced out along each hall—one by each exhibit room's doorway, one by each bathroom door and then inside each bathroom, and one by each office door as well. Those should help a lot!

With the knowledge that their emergency lights were in good hands, and Randall bellowing at them to fall in line and Bud chittering excitedly, Malik and the others assembled behind their teacher. They climbed back up the stairs outside the museum, into the museum proper. Then Mr. Enright led them down a long hall they hadn't used yet, past several other exhibit rooms, and finally to a large, open room filled with long tables and benches.

"Is this the cafeteria?" Chris asked. "Because I'm starving!" He rubbed his stomach as if to prove the point.

"It is," their teacher answered. "Normally you can buy food and drinks here while you're visiting the museum. Right now, of course, the refrigerators, freezers, and ovens have no power. But that doesn't mean nothing is working." He gestured dramatically toward one wall, where a row of glass-fronted counters stood. It was clearly where the museum normally served its food. "Behold!"

Approaching the counters, Malik saw that the stainless steel trays that should have held food were not, in fact, empty. "What're those?" he asked, pointing at the strange metal boxes standing in each tray. The top of each box looked similar to an oven burner.

"Those are the camp stoves I mentioned last night," Mr. Enright replied. "Remember? They're a lot like tiny grills, and you only need a single Sterno can for each one." He leaned around the farthest counter, and when he straightened up again he was holding a large box, which he then opened to reveal a pile of Sterno cans. "Voila!"

"Is it safe to use these indoors?" Chris asked as they all rounded the counters to study the little black stoves.

"It is," their teacher promised, "especially if you keep it away from anything else flammable and you have decent ventilation." He indicated the large windows at the room's far end, which were wide open. And of course the camp stoves were sitting in metal trays, Malik thought, so that was good.

"Open the front like you would a little cabinet, and then I'll light each can and you can slide it inside," Mr. Enright instructed as he handed each of them a can. "Once we have them going, we'll get out the food. Each can will stay lit for hours, so we might be able to cook breakfast tomorrow morning on them as well, if that's necessary. I believe I have enough food to cover that possibility." He gestured toward several coolers lined up behind them. Apparently their teacher had been pretty busy!

"What're we having?" Malik asked with a grin as he stationed himself in front of one of the little square stoves. "Because if it's chicken cordon bleu, I don't have the recipe handy."

"How do hot dogs sound?" their teacher replied. "I figured those were easy to cook and tasty, and almost everybody likes them. And we've got tofu dogs too, for the vegetarians—we'll designate one or two of the stoves for those, so there won't be any risk of them getting mixed up."

"Sounds good to me!" Chris said, and this time they all heard his stomach grumble. "See?" That got them all laughing.

But Ilyana had a question. "We aren't just making food for ourselves, are we?" she asked, flicking her long hair back over her shoulder. "I mean, I appreciate it and all, but what about everyone else? They've got to be getting hungry too!" Malik felt a little guilty that he hadn't thought about the rest of the students as well. He knew each of the teachers had brought sandwiches for today's lunch—Mr. Enright had distributed theirs to them while they were still at the AERIE—but the original plan had been for the museum cafeteria to provide dinner.

"Not to worry," Mr. Enright assured them all. "I made sure to purchase an ample supply. We will cook a sufficient quantity for all, then travel around and inform the other classes that dinner is served!"

That made Malik feel a lot better. Ilyana was clearly pleased as well, and they were all laughing and talking and joking as they got their little camp stoves ready. Once the Sterno cans were in place, cheery blue flames rose from within each burner, and then Mr. Enright handed them a small metal grilling rack. Those went over the burners, and then the hot dogs were laid out across those. Malik had helped his dad grill plenty of times, so he was perfectly comfortable with that part of the process.

"Imagine everybody else's surprise once they start smelling the food," Jules said while they were waiting for the hot dogs to heat up. "It'll drive them crazy trying to figure out what's going on!"

"And then they'll step out into the halls and they'll actually be able to see where they're going," Malik added. "That'll be pretty cool, too." He actually had no idea what the other science classes had been doing all day. Had they each migrated to outer rooms, where they'd at least have sunlight and fresh air? Or were they all still huddled in the exhibit rooms they'd been assigned, even if those were interior spaces and had no natural lighting? He shivered at the idea of just sitting around in the dark all day. Good thing STEM1 was on the case!

CHAPTER 21

SOMETHING IN MY EYE

Ever since she'd gotten up that morning, Jules had had something on her mind. Or, more specifically, someone.

Randall.

That prank he'd played on them last night, sneaking up and scaring them in the dark? Not cool. Not cool at all.

And something like that demanded payback.

The problem was, how would she get back at him?

She thought about their teacher's aide. What did she really know about him? He was in college and was in ROTC. He wanted to go into the Navy, specifically the SEALs. He was super gung ho about anything military and liked to act as if they were all in boot camp and he was their training sergeant. He wanted to go into demolitions. And he already knew how to use night vision goggles. Really well, in fact.

But wait. She paused as a thought struck her. He might know how to use them, but how much did he know about how they worked? Probably no more than the rest of them, and that was only because Mr. Enright had explained it to them after he'd handed the goggles out last night.

Which meant there were plenty of things about the goggles Randall didn't know.

Or things he didn't know weren't true.

A plan started to form in her mind. But to pull it off, she was going to need a little help.

The first person she asked was Tracey. Of course her friend was in. "Pay back that slug for freaking us out in the dark?" she asked. "Heck yeah!" And then Jules told her what she was thinking. "Awesome!" Her friend laughed. "But what about the others?"

Jules grinned. "That's who I'm talking to next."

She went to Malik next. She had a feeling he'd be up for it—she knew Randall got on his nerves too. Sure enough, he was all over the idea. "Oh, we can totally sell this!" he agreed enthusiastically. "Ha, and I've got just the thing for it!" He told her what he'd packed, and Jules laughed, shaking her head. Leave it to a clotheshorse like Malik to be prepared for anything, even a prank!

Chris said sure, it sounded like fun and Randall certainly deserved it. It wasn't like they were going to hurt the guy or anything, anyway—just mess with him a little bit.

Ilyana was the one Jules wasn't sure about. Out of all their class, she was the most tenderhearted. Which is why Jules was surprised that Ilyana immediately agreed to the plan.

"He's just so full of himself," Ilyana explained, brushing back her long hair. "He needs to be taken down a peg or two. It'll be good for him."

Leave it to someone like Ilyana to find a way to make a prank into a lesson!

Everyone was onboard, so it was all good. Now they just had to get everything into place.

That turned out to be easy enough too. Once all the Sterno cans were lit and the hot dogs were starting to cook, Mr. Enright stepped out in front of the counters to address them all.

"Looking good, STEM class!" their teacher told them. "I think we're just about ready here. The dogs will take a few minutes, so if you wanted to hit the bathrooms, freshen up, or even just relax for a bit, this would be a good time."

Jules glanced around. Tracey caught her eye and nodded. Malik winked. Chris and Ilyana both smirked. And Randall?

Randall stayed ramrod-straight at his camping stove, like a guard assigned to watch some precious treasure.

Perfect.

"Yeah, I could use a walk," Jules declared, stretching. "To the exhibit room and back, maybe."

"Totally," Tracey agreed. "Stretch our legs, work out the kinks."

Malik nodded. "Sounds good to me." Chris and Ilyana chimed in as well.

"We'll be right back," Jules assured Mr. Enright, who was studying them with one eyebrow raised. Clearly he could tell something was going on, but he just wasn't sure what. Still, he nodded, and Jules didn't stick around to see if he had any questions or changed his mind. She immediately headed for the door, her classmates right behind her.

Once they were back in their exhibit room, everyone started pulling out clothes. It took them a few minutes to get ready, especially since they had to work in shifts. Fortunately, the bathrooms were just down the hall. When they were done, they headed back to the cafeteria. Randall was still on guard, but Mr. Enright was nowhere in sight.

Perfect.

"Man, I am so relieved," Jules declared loudly as they approached the counters. "I was a little worried— it's hard to tell in the dark, you know?"

The others all nodded. "Yeah, and my shirt was dark anyway," Tracey agreed. She'd been wearing a wine-red T-shirt before. "That would've sucked."

Randall glared at them. "What would've sucked?" he demanded, clearly annoyed at being left out of something.

"Hmm?" Jules frowned at him, then shrugged. "Oh, nothing—just something we'd heard about with those night vision goggles Mr. Enright gave us last night."

Their teacher's aide smirked at them. "Still haven't figured out how to use those, huh?" he practically sneered.

The crack made Jules seethe inside, but she forced herself to act calm. This wouldn't work otherwise.

"Oh, nothing like that," she answered, pleased that she still sounded totally relaxed, even relieved. "It was just, well, you know. The whole photoreceptor thing."

A **photoreceptor** is a specialized cell that responds to light. The rods and cones in a person's retina are photoreceptors.

Now Randall looked confused. "What photoreceptor thing?" And was that a trace of worry creeping into her voice?

At her side, Malik nodded. "Yeah, I looked it up after you mentioned it," he declared, holding up his phone. "Good thing I was able to recharge at AERIE! Anyway, it's pretty nasty, but I guess we weren't wearing them long enough to be affected."

"Wait, what?" Randall definitely sounded concerned now, and he leaned so far forward that Jules worried his shirt might catch fire from the camp stove in front of him.

"You know," she replied, "the photoreceptors—how too much night vision can damage them."

Randall was eyeing them all suspiciously, but he was also sweating a little, Jules saw. "What exactly happens to them?" he asked, his voice wavering a little.

"Oh, they say colors are the first to go," Chris offered.

Ilyana nodded. "Yeah, everything goes black and white and gray." She shuddered. "That would be awful!"

"I know, right?" Jules told her. She tapped her T-shirt. "Like this would be gray instead of bright blue? Ugh!"

"What? Bright blue?" Randall stared at her, eyes wide. Yep, definitely sweating now.

"Yeah, even a Day-Glo yellow like this one wouldn't show up anymore," Malik added, pulling the sleeve of his own shirt. He grinned. "Though I guess that'd make picking clothes a lot easier, if they all looked like they matched."

Randall was gaping at them now. His eyes flicked from shirt to shirt. He even glanced down at his own clothes, but of course he was wearing black head to toe, like usual. He looked like he was going to cry. "My eyes!" he shouted, scrubbing at them. "They're ruined!"

Abandoning his post, Randall ran for the door. Mr. Enright was just coming in from the hall, and the two of them nearly collided. Randall stopped for a second, staring up at the tall STEM teacher, who Jules hadn't even realized was wearing a light gray button-down shirt, a dark gray tie, and dark gray slacks. "It's getting worse!" Randall declared, and he bolted from the room.

Mr. Enright watched him go and then turned back to study his students. "Is there something going on I should know about?" he asked gently. He frowned. "And is there a reason you have all gone monochromatic suddenly?"

That one had Jules confused, and most of her friends too by the looks on their faces, until Ilyana explained. "Monochrome is one color," she told the rest of them. "And a lot of times people use that when they really mean black and white."

"Oh." Jules nodded. "It was a joke," she told their teacher. She gestured at her friends. "We were paying Randall back for something he did to us last night. He'll be fine."

"And hopping mad once he sees something in color again!" Malik added, laughing.

That got Jules giggling, remembering the look on Randall's face. Then Tracey started chortling, and soon they were all laughing. In between, Jules managed to explain to their teacher what they'd done.

"Well," he said when she'd finished. "I applaud your ingenuity, certainly. And you are correct; he should not have startled you last night." Then

193

he laughed. "Perhaps this will teach him to show more respect in the future. Or at least not to believe everything he hears—or sees!"

Shaking his head, their teacher walked away. And Jules turned to her classmates.

"Thanks, guys," she told them. "I couldn't have done it without you."

"Are you kidding?" Malik replied. "That was a blast!" He laughed. "I'm just glad I packed extra shirts! And that they were all monochrome!"

That had been the key, of course. They'd all changed into shirts that were black, white, or gray.

"Good thing Randall didn't think to look down," Chris commented as they wandered back behind the counters to check on the food. "Or he might have known we were tricking him." He pointed at his camp stove, and Jules gulped. Chris was right—the flames from the Sterno can were still a brilliant blue, and the hot dogs themselves were a juicy-looking pink. But Randall had been so focused on their clothes that he hadn't thought to check that. Whew!

"Maybe we should get him a special gray hot dog, just to complete the picture," Malik suggested, eliciting another round of chuckles. But no, Jules was already satisfied. She'd had her revenge.

CHAPTER 22

OPEN MOUTH, INSERT FOOT

"Dinner!" Malik announced as he poked his head into the room Mrs. Cavanaugh's class occupied. "Dinner is served! Come on down to the cafeteria and get some dinner!"

Mrs. Cavanaugh turned to study him, and Chris behind him. "Do you mean to say that someone has prepared food for all of us?" she asked, aiming her flashlight at their faces.

"Yep," he agreed, raising one hand to shield his eyes from the light. "Us. The STEM class. We made dinner for everybody. It's in the cafeteria."

Malik's friend Jay was already on his feet. "Sweet—I'm starved!" he declared. Then he paused. "Wait, where's the cafeteria?"

"Take a right, head straight down the hall, and hang another right at the end," Chris told him and the rest of the students. "You can't miss it."

"But it's dark," one of the other kids complained.

"We can't see where we're going!"

"Sure you can," Malik replied. "Come on, take a look." He and Chris backed out of the doorway, and the class followed them—and gasped when they saw the emergency lights lining the hallway. "See?"

Some of the kids clapped, a few cheered, another whistled. Even Mrs. Cavanaugh sighed happily. "This is a pleasant surprise!" she announced. "All right, class, follow me!" And she led the way down the hall.

Malik smiled and watched them go, then he turned to Chris. "Next?" he said.

"Down the hall and to the left," his friend replied. Together they continued on their way. Mr. Enright had divided them up into groups to find the other science classes and let them know that dinner was ready, and this time he'd let Chris and Malik stay as a duo, while Jules, Tracey, and Ilyana were the other team. Each group had two classes to speak to, so once they told the next class that dinner was ready, they could head back and get some food themselves. Malik wasn't too worried—Mr. Enright had promised that they'd have plenty for everyone.

By the time they got back to the cafeteria, it was a madhouse—in a good way. The tables were lined with students, and everyone was eating and talking and laughing. Malik saw plenty of kids he knew and called out and waved to people as he and Chris made a beeline for the food counters.

"Ah, the triumphant guides return," Mr. Enright announced from his station by the camp stoves. He smiled and lifted two paper plates, each one packed with two hot dogs and a pile of potato chips. He handed each of them a plate and then reached down and offered them each a bottle of water as well. "Condiments are at the end," he explained, gesturing toward the far end of the counters, where Malik saw packets of ketchup, mustard, relish, and even mayonnaise.

"Awesome, thanks." Malik took his food and glanced around. Off to one side, he spotted Jules, Tracey, and Ilyana around a table that still had plenty of space. They waved him and Chris over. "Come on," Malik told his friend, elbowing him to get his attention. Then they went and joined the girls, who had obviously beaten them back by several minutes if their half-empty plates were any indication.

"Man, it's amazing how, after even just one day without power, something as simple as a hot dog can taste gourmet!" Tracey said as they all ate. Malik nodded, his mouth too full to speak. She was right, though—just having hot food seemed like a luxury now. And he could tell, from the sounds they were hearing all around them, that the other kids agreed, and not just the ones in STEM1.

The students weren't the only ones who were grateful. Several of the other teachers stopped by to thank the STEM class for everything they'd done. And after them came Dr. Pillai.

"I have to say, I'm impressed," their school principal informed them. "Not only did you all keep your heads during the blackout, but you also managed to set up this meal for everyone, which is incredibly nice of you and has done wonders for easing any fears and concerns. Nice job."

The kids all beamed at the praise.

"We're also incredibly lucky that Mr. Enright was able to get in touch with his friends at the Alternative Energy Research Institute," Dr. Pillai added as their teacher joined them, sliding his long legs over the far end of one bench and setting a plate of his own on the table. "And I know Ms. Dancy feels the same way."

All the kids nodded.

"Plus," Malik blurted out after he'd swallowed his latest bite of hot dog, "that place is killer! Seriously, it's amazing!"

Then he froze, as did the other kids. And Mr. Enright. And Dr. Pillai swiveled to stare at him.

"What do you mean," she demanded. "The

institute? How would you know what it looks like?" Then, eyes narrowing, she shifted to glare at their teacher, who suddenly found his food extremely interesting.

"You took them to the institute?" their principal accused, her voice a steely hiss. "You drove there with them? During a blackout? Do you realize how dangerous that is, with all the traffic lights down?"

"It wasn't that bad," Tracey offered. "The cops were really nice about it."

"The cops?" Dr. Pillai looked like her head was about to explode. "You promised me," she reminded Mr. Enright. "You swore that you wouldn't let these kids come to any harm, that you would make sure they stayed safe, that you wouldn't take any more unnecessary risks—"

"—and I have upheld that promise," their teacher interrupted, finally looking up and meeting the principal's eyes. "I have kept them safe—not a single one of them has been harmed. As Tracey said, the police were perfectly content that we were behaving in a safe fashion. Which we were. We were careful. Everyone is fine. And the museum will soon have light, and power, and water. And we have hot food." He held up his plate to her like it was a peace offering. "Here," he suggested. "Have another hot dog."

For a second, the principal just stared at him, evidently rendered speechless. Then she turned and stomped away.

But not before snatching one of the hot dogs off Mr. Enright's plate.

"She'll calm down," their teacher assured them once she'd left the table. "She always does." He gazed forlornly at the now empty spot on his plate and then glanced back toward the food counter and perked up. "In the meantime," he said, swinging his legs back around and standing up, "would anyone care for another hot dog?"

"Come by again some time," Dr. Deere told them as he and his crew prepared to depart. "There's still plenty of stuff we didn't have time to show you."

"We definitely will," Mr. Enright promised. "And thanks again, Don." The two men shook hands, and then the AERIE team headed out, back to their vans and then to their institute.

Ms. Dancy had returned just as they'd all been filing out of the cafeteria, and now she made her way over to Mr. Enright and the STEM class. "I can't thank you enough," she told them all. "We're so grateful for everything you've done."

"You're quite welcome," Mr. Enright told her. He smiled. "And once those solar panels get a few days to charge, you should never have to worry about losing power no matter what happens outside. This museum will be a safe, well-lit place for everyone, old and young alike, to come and learn."

The museum curator beamed at him.

And just as she did—the lights came back on!

"Yay!" everyone cheered.

"Right," Dr. Pillai announced. "Teachers, back to your assigned rooms. The power's back on, so let's make the most of it!"

"Just think," Mr. Enright commented as he led his class toward their room, "in a few days these halls will never be truly dark again!"

Behind him, Randall groaned. "No more stealth ops?" he asked.

"Look on the bright side, Randall," Jules called out from her place in line. "At least this way your eyesight will be safe!"

The teacher's aide growled at her, while the rest of them all laughed. Even Mr. Enright.

All in all, Malik decided that this had been a pretty amazing weekend. They'd done a lot, and learned a lot, and helped out a lot.

Which wasn't a surprise, because they always had a fun time—and an educational one—in STEM class!

STUDY GUIDE
Quiz

Okay, so you've finished reading the book. Congratulations! Now, how much of it do you remember? See how well you do on the following quiz—and no cheating and flipping back to figure out the answers (found on page 206)!

1. In Chapter One, what is Jules excited about doing tomorrow?

   a. Going to a dance
   b. Going on a field trip
   c. Going to the store
   d. Going to the moon

2. What happens while she's packing?

   a. The air conditioning turns on.
   b. The lights go out.
   c. The lights flicker.
   d. The ceiling fan comes to life.

3. Why did Jules's father invite their old neighbor over?

   a. To talk about Jules's game
   b. To have a picnic
   c. To check their home's wiring
   d. To help with a jigsaw puzzle

4. At school who does Malik run into—literally?

   a. Bud, his chimp pal
   b. Mr. Enright, his science teacher
   c. Kilam, his evil twin
   d. Kevin, his classmate

5. What is the problem
   with the buses?

   a. Not enough gas
   b. Not enough space
   c. Not enough light
   d. Not enough bubblegum

6. What is the focus of the
   exhibit room the STEM
   class is staying in?

   a. Kites
   b. Cats
   c. Light
   d. Bones

7. What happens while
   they're in the room?

   a. The exhibits attack.
   b. The floor gives way.
   c. The food arrives.
   d. The lights go out.

8. What does Mr. Enright
   hand out to his students?

   a. Night vision goggles
   b. X-ray glasses
   c. Oversized sunglasses
   d. Opera glasses

9. Who pulls a nasty surprise
   on Jules and Tracey?

   a. Bud
   b. Dr. Pillai
   c. Malik
   d. Randall

10. What is Kevin trapped
    within?

    a. The bathroom
    b. His sleeping bag
    c. A supply closet
    d. A dinosaur skeleton

11. Why does Mr. Enright's
    phone still work during
    the blackout?

    a. He charged it
       beforehand.
    b. It comes with an
       extension cord.
    c. It's a satellite phone.
    d. He's calling collect.

12. Who stops their school
    bus?

    a. The police
    b. The FBI
    c. The military
    d. The Girl Scouts

13. Who runs the Alternative Energy Research Institute?

a. Dr. Moose
b. Dr. Foxe
c. Dr. Lambe
d. Dr. Deere

14. Which of these is a renewable resource?

a. Oil
b. Wind
c. Gas
d. Coal

15. How long have photovoltaic cells been around?

a. Since the 1980s
b. Since the 1580s
c. Since the 1850s
d. Since the 2580s

16. What does Roy G. Biv stand for?

a. The days of the week
b. The months of the year
c. The points of the compass
d. The colors of the rainbow

17. Which was used for energy first?

a. Wind
b. Sun
c. Oil
d. Oregano

18. What do kinetic tiles do?

a. Convert feet to meters
b. Convert dollars to pounds
c. Convert footsteps to electricity
d. Convert solids to liquids

19. What are the AERIE and the STEM kids going to do to the museum?

a. Make it bulletproof
b. Make it waterproof
c. Make it earthquake-proof
d. Make it blackout-proof

20. What do they put on the museum roof?

a. A sundial
b. Solar panels
c. A sunshade
d. Sunscreen

21. What doesn't work at first?

   a. The elevator
   b. The escalator
   c. The exit sign
   d. The emergency lights

22. What's the problem with them?

   a. Not enough current
   b. Not enough light
   c. Not enough space
   d. Not enough hot sauce

23. What is Mr. Enright's surprise for the class?

   a. They're going to paint the halls.
   b. They're going to wash the windows.
   c. They're going to sweep the floors.
   d. They're going to prepare lunch.

24. How do the kids mess with Randall?

   a. They pretend he's going tone-deaf.
   b. They pretend he's going color-blind.
   c. They pretend he's going cross-eyed.
   d. They pretend he's going to turn into a gorilla.

25. What does Dr. Pillai steal from Mr. Enright?

   a. His tie
   b. His hat
   c. His watch
   d. His dinner

Quiz Answer Key

1. b	10. d	19. d
2. c	11. c	20. b
3. c	12. a	21. d
4. d	13. d	22. a
5. b	14. b	23. d
6. c	15. c	24. b
7. d	16. d	25. d
8. a	17. a	
9. d	18. c	

Discussion Questions

Here are a few questions you can discuss with your class about what happened in the book and why. These are less about remembering specific details or finding answers and more about sharing your own thoughts, ideas, and feelings about the characters and the story—and the science!

1. Why is Jules scared when the lights flicker? Would you be? Why or why not?

2. Do you think it would be fun to sleep at a museum? Why or why not?

3. If you could visit any one room at the natural history museum, which would it be? Why? If you had to sleep in the museum, would you pick that same room or a different one?

4. What do you think would be the worst part of being stuck in a blackout?

5. Does your family have food, water, and other necessities set aside in case of a blackout or other disaster? Do you think people should, or is that overreacting?

6. Do you think it would be fun or scary to wear night vision goggles? What would be the hardest thing about using them?

7. If sat phones work so much better than regular cell phones, why do you think everyone doesn't have a sat phone instead?

8. Do you think it's irresponsible of Mr. Enright to take the class out during a blackout? Would you risk riding in a car during one?

9. Which of the renewable resources at the AERIE did you think was the coolest? Why?

10. Which renewable resource is the most useful, in your opinion? Which one should we be focusing our attention on developing further?

11. Do you agree that we should switch entirely to renewable energy? Or should we continue to use nonrenewable resources for some—or all—of our energy needs? Why?

12. Would you put solar panels on your house if you could? Wind turbines? Kinetic tiles? Why or why not?

13. There are other ways to conserve energy that the book doesn't cover. Can you think of any?

14. What about other forms of renewable energy? What did the book leave out?

15. One thing the AERIE and the STEM kids do is add a water filtration system so the museum can use—and even drink—rainwater. Do you think that's weird? Would you be okay with drinking filtered rainwater? What about recycling the water you use in your home—like in the shower? Or the toilet?

16. Do you think people are taking the energy problem seriously enough? Or too seriously? Is there anything the government could be doing that it isn't already?

17. Do rolling blackouts and brownouts really work? Do you think they teach people to be more careful about how much energy they use every day? Is there anything else we could do to better educate people on proper energy usage?

18. Where do you think would be the worst place in the world to have a blackout? Where would be the easiest place to endure it?

19. What about the worst weather to be without power? Would it be worse to have no power during a thunderstorm, for example, or a blizzard or drought?

20. If you had to give up one thing that uses electricity, what would it be? What's the one thing you couldn't give up?

21. What do you think of Jules's prank on Randall? Did he deserve it?

22. Is there anything Ms. Dancy could do to make the museum even more energy-efficient?

23. What was the most useful thing you learned from the story?

24. Which of the careers featured in the story would you be most interested in doing? Why?

25. Where do you think the class will go next?

STEM Careers

The STEM kids meet several grown-ups who have STEM-based careers. Here's a little more about each of those jobs, including what you need in order to get one!

AEROSPACE ENGINEER: Aerospace engineers work on the theory and practice of aerodynamics, or how things move through the air—and how the air moves around them. Most aerospace engineers work on developing aircraft or even spacecraft, but some work as wind engineers instead. These engineers study wind turbines, working on ways to improve their efficiency by developing better blades and rotors. They also help find the best locations for wind farms and where and how to best set up turbines on commercial and even residential sites. Becoming an aerospace engineer requires a degree from one of the country's aerospace engineering programs, followed by a Professional Engineering license.

ELECTRICAL ENGINEER: An electrical engineer installs and checks electrical components in homes and other buildings. They also research, design, and test electrical equipment for commercial, industrial, military, or scientific use. To be an electrical engineer you need a bachelor's degree in electrical engineering and certification as a Professional Engineer.

GEOCHEMIST: Geochemists investigate the amount and balance of chemicals in rocks and minerals. They also study how those chemicals move through soil and water, and the composition of fossil fuel deposits. Geochemists can help improve water quality, clean up toxic waste sites, locate and develop mining sites, and set up and maintain geothermal plants. Most geochemists have a degree in geology and a related field such as chemical engineering, marine sciences, or mining engineering.

LAB WORKERS: At the bottom level are the lab assistants, who help do basic laboratory testing by collecting samples, managing inventory, and cleaning lab equipment. Above them are the lab technicians, who run most of the actual experiments. And ranked highest are lab technologists, who run the labs for the scientists and oversee both the lab assistants and lab technicians.

METALLURGIST: Although the STEM class didn't meet a metallurgist directly, there were probably a few at the AERIE. Metallurgists study the properties of metals and how to put them to the best use. For example, a metallurgist would work with Dr. Buchannan to create solar cells made from different metals. A metallurgist would also work with Dr. Chang to create wind turbine blades from other metals or metal alloys to produce lighter, stronger, less expensive blades. These would be process metallurgists, meaning metallurgists who design metal equipment and objects and test their use. There are also chemical metallurgists, who test ores and study how to extract metal, test it for quality, and strengthen it, and physical metallurgists, who study how metals handle physical stress. To be a metallurgist you need a degree in materials science or engineering and a license as a Professional Engineer.

MUSEUM CURATOR: Museum curators are responsible for overseeing a museum's collections. That means acquiring pieces, authenticating them (making sure the pieces are real), preserving them, and displaying them. Curators also help with fundraising, public relations, and management. To be a curator you need at least a college degree, but most have a master's degree or even a doctorate in the area they want to work in, such as history or art. Most curators start out by interning at a museum and then move up to being an assistant or a research associate so they can get job experience.

SOLAR ENGINEER: Solar engineers plan, design, build, and install solar energy projects. They work on everything from citywide projects to individual home installations. You better not be afraid of heights if you want this job— solar engineers are often on rooftops, installing solar panels! Most solar engineers have a bachelor's degree in mechanical engineering or electrical engineering. Some also have degrees in industrial engineering, chemical engineering, or computer software engineering. You also need to be licensed as an Engineer in Training and then eventually as a Professional Engineer.

STEM Tools

The kids in STEM class get to hear about, see, and even play with some cool gadgets. Here's a list:

MULTIMETER: A tool electricians use to measure electrical current, voltage, and resistance. Most multimeters have a clamp or gap at the top so that you can simply slip them around a wire in order to get a reading.

NIGHT VISION GOGGLES: Special goggles that use a combination of lenses and other equipment to take in ambient light and magnify it, allowing the wearer to effectively see in the dark as long as there is even a little light available.

SAT PHONE: Sat phones, or satellite phones, are mobile phones that connect directly to orbiting satellites instead of local cellular towers. This means that a sat phone will work anywhere in the world, as long as it's out in the open and there's at least one communications satellite somewhere in orbit.

SOLAR PANELS: Wide, flat panels of solar cells designed to be set up outside (preferably on a rooftop) where they can absorb solar energy and convert it to electricity.

KINETIC TILES: Special floor tiles that absorb the kinetic energy from a footstep and convert it to electricity.

CHALK LINE: This is actually a very old and fairly low-tech device, but an extremely useful one for builders! It's a coiled-up cord inside a small case equipped with a crank handle. When you pull out the cord, the case coats it in chalk. You tighten the cord with the crank so that when you press the line onto a flat surface, it leaves blue chalk in a straight line.

LIGHT SENSOR: A tiny sensor that detects the light level around it. It is most often used for outdoor lights and emergency lights that only turn on when it gets dark.

STERNO CAN: A small can filled with Sterno, a fuel made from jellied alcohol. When lit, it provides a low but steady flame, perfect for light cooking duties or for keeping food warm on a buffet line.

Museum Overnight Programs

Did you read about the STEM kids going on an overnight field trip to a museum and say, "No way, museums don't do that!" Guess what? They really do! Here are some museums that have overnight programs. If none of these are near you, check out your local museums. Maybe they have overnight stays available too!

AMERICAN MUSEUM OF NATURAL HISTORY, NEW YORK, NEW YORK

It's just like the hit movie *A Night at the Museum*, as you're taken through the halls and among the dinosaurs! See a live animal exhibition by the Audubon Society, watch a 3-D movie or space show, make some crafts, and sleep beneath the museum's famous big blue whale! Sleepovers run from 5:45 p.m. to 9 a.m. and include an evening snack and a light breakfast. Cots are provided, but kids need to bring their own sleeping bags, pillows, and flashlights. This event is open to kids 6 to 13 years of age, and there must be at least one adult for every three children.

CARNEGIE SCIENCE CENTER, PITTSBURGH, PENNSYLVANIA

Monthly themed sleepovers start at 6 p.m. and end at 9:30 a.m. and include live shows, an Omnimax movie, theme-related activities, and time to explore the other exhibits. Bring a sleeping bag and a pillow and sleep anywhere there's carpet! The sleepover is open to kids 4 to 10 years of age and requires at least one adult for every eight children. A late-night snack and breakfast are included.

CINCINNATI MUSEUM CENTER, CINCINNATI, OHIO

Choose from two different overnight programs at this museum complex—with caves! You'll learn about bats, beetles, and other nocturnal life at the limestone caves in the Museum of Natural History & Science. With the "Explore!" program, you'll wander around both the natural history facility and the Cincinnati History Museum. For both museum visits, sleepovers start at 7 p.m. and end at 10 a.m.; they include an Omnimax movie in the morning. They're open to kids 8 to 12 years of age and require one adult for every four children.

DENVER MUSEUM OF NATURE AND SCIENCE, DENVER, COLORADO

Learn about space, health, science, and nature through interactive exhibits and IMAX films on this overnight stay. It's for kids 6 to 13 years of age in families or groups of six or more, and it includes admission to the Denver Zoo the next day. There's also a planetarium show, an evening snack, and a light breakfast. The overnight runs from 6 p.m. to 11 a.m.

INTERNATIONAL SPY MUSEUM, WASHINGTON, D.C.

Become a secret agent for the special overnight program, "KidSpy Overnight: Operation Secret Slumber." Kids 9 to 13 years of age choose aliases, create disguises, learn new identities, and then work together to compete with the adults at decoding messages, finding dead drops, and discovering the mole in your group. One adult is required for every two children.

MILWAUKEE PUBLIC MUSEUM, MILWAUKEE, WISCONSIN

Explore the museum during these themed overnight events. Each overnight includes a planetarium show or giant-screen movie, discovery hunts, self-guided flashlight tours, and educator-led hands-on activities. The overnights are open to kids 6 to 12 years of age, and one adult is required for every five children. The overnights start at 6 p.m. and end at 8 a.m. A light evening snack and breakfast are provided.

MUSEUM OF SCIENCE, BOSTON, MASSACHUSETTS

Groups of 10 or more can spend the night surrounded by science, exploring exhibits after-hours and enjoying presentations, activities, shows, and demonstrations. The overnights are for kids 7 to 12 years of age and start at 6:45 p.m. and end at 11 a.m. They include snacks and breakfast.

MUSEUM OF SCIENCE AND INDUSTRY, CHICAGO, ILLINOIS

Groups of 10 or more can enjoy a "Science Snoozeum" and sleep beneath a 727, near a giant heart or beside a toy-making factory. You'll also get to explore the museum, take part in a scavenger hunt, and watch an Omnimax film. The overnight starts at 5:30 p.m. and ends at 8:30 a.m. It is open to kids 6 to 12 years of age and requires one parent for every five children. Snacks and breakfast are included.

NATIONAL BASEBALL HALL OF FAME AND MUSEUM, COOPERSTOWN, NEW YORK

Get a private screening of the Baseball Experience, try out activity stations at several exhibits, and explore the museum after-hours, then bed down in the Hall of Fame Gallery and other selected spaces. The overnight is open to kids 7 to 12 years of age. It starts at 6:30 p.m. Saturday and ends at 8 a.m. Sunday. An evening snack, a light breakfast, and a souvenir knapsack are provided.

NATURAL HISTORY MUSEUM, LOS ANGELES, CALIFORNIA

Experience a themed "Overnight Adventures" program, such as "Camp Dinosaur," "Camp Butterfly," or "Camp Mummies." These overnights are for kids 5 years of age and older. They start at 7 p.m. and end at 9 a.m. and include museum admission the next day. Snacks and a light breakfast are provided.

ST. LOUIS SCIENCE CENTER, ST. LOUIS, MISSOURI

Enjoy a themed overnight stay that includes an Omnimax film, science demonstrations, activities, a planetarium show, and time to explore the rest of the museum. The themed programs include "Dinosaurs in Motion," "Planetarium," and "Sherlock Holmes." These overnights are open to kids 6 years of age and older, with one adult required for every five children. They start at 5 p.m. and end at 10 a.m. A pizza dinner, snacks, and breakfast are provided.

Additional Resources

Want to learn more about blackouts, more about alternate energy sources, more about the careers mentioned in the book, or just more about STEM in general? Here are a few places you can find additional information:

The Solar Energy Industries Association (SEIA)
www.seia.org

The Association of Energy Engineers
www.aeecenter.org

The Institute of Electrical and Electronics Engineers (IEEE)
www.ieee.org

Environmental Science.org
www.environmentalscience.org

How Stuff Works: How Blackouts Work
science.howstuffworks.com/environmental/energy/blackout.htm

The Energy Dictionary: Blackout, Brownout, Brown Power, and Rolling Blackout
www.energyvortex.com/energydictionary/blackout__ brownout__brown_power__rolling_blackout.html

(#310) 7/16